SMALL
SHADOWS
CREEP

SMALL SHADOWS CREEP

compiled by

ANDRE NORTON

E. P. DUTTON & CO., INC.   NEW YORK

LIBRARY OF CONGRESS CATALOGING IN PUBLICATION DATA

Norton, Andre, comp.   Small shadows creep

CONTENTS: Ancient evils: Lawrence, M.   Saloozy.
Munby, A. B. L.   Herodes redivivus.
Wakefield, H. R.   The first sheaf. [etc.]

1. Ghost stories. [1. Ghost stories. 2. Supernatural—
Fiction]   I. Title.
PZ5.N65Sm   823′.0872   [Fic]   74–5408   ISBN 0–525–39505–9

Published simultaneously in Canada by Clarke,
Irwin & Company Limited, Toronto and Vancouver

Designed by Meri Shardin
Printed in the U.S.A.   First Edition
10 9 8 7 6 5 4 3 2 1

ACKNOWLEDGMENTS

We gratefully acknowledge permission to reprint the following copyright material:

"Saloozy" by Margery Lawrence, from *Master of Shadows*. Reprinted by permission of David Higham Associates, Ltd.

"Herodes Redivivus" by A. N. L. Munby, from *The Alabaster Hand*. Reprinted by permission of Dobson Books, London.

"The First Sheaf" by H. R. Wakefield, from *The Clock Strikes Twelve*. Reprinted by permission of Arkham House, Sauk City, Wisconsin.

"How Fear Departed from the Long Gallery" by E. F. Benson, from *The Room in the Tower*. Reprinted by permission of The Estate of E. F. Benson.

"Lost Hearts" by M. R. James, from *Collected Ghost Stories*. Reprinted by permission of Edward Arnold Publishers, Ltd.

"A Little Ghost" by Hugh Walpole, from *When Churchyards Yawn*. Reprinted by permission of Sir Rupert Hart-Davis.

"Playmates" by A. M. Burrage, from *Some Ghost Stories*. Reprinted by permission of Stephen Aske, Literary Agent.

"Faithful Jenny Dove" by Eleanor Farjeon, from *Faithful Jenny Dove*. Reprinted by permission of David Higham Associates, Ltd.

INTRODUCTION

"From ghoulies and ghosties and long-legged beasties
And things that go bump in the Night
Good Lord, deliver us!"

In the ancient days though people of the countryside repeated such counterspells as these, yet they loved stories of those same ghoulies and ghosties. Black Dog Shuck ran dark lanes at midnight for the unlucky traveler to meet. In the midst of wild autumn storms Herne the Hunter led his mad crew across country, and woeful indeed was the fate of those who saw *them!*

Shuck and Herne were old, old things out of the misty past, and became so worn in the telling that they no longer raised shudders. Then masters of tale-making began to create their own ghostly visitants for the frightening of kinsmen or neighbors.

Ghosts must, of course, have the proper settings in which to appear. We can readily accept a Grey Lady or a headless horseman or a Black Monk where ruined buildings show broken teeth of walls against a half-clouded moon. But a ghost who pads—or clanks dismally—along the hallways of a modern apartment—NO!

The nineteenth and the very early years of the present century brought us ghosts to the very best patterns. Certainly their like will never be seen again—for their haunts have become parking lots and supermarkets—if not worse. We have destroyed the stages on which they appeared with the bulldozer and all the rest of modern clutter.

Therefore to savor the best in shakes and quivers one must return to books thirty, forty, fifty, eighty years old.

Recently it was my task to check through a collection of such volumes to list the tales included. And that task impressed me with the fact that many of the most telling and exciting stories in these books (now largely long out of print) dealt with children and young people whom the evil or twilight half-world had captured for better or worse.

So here is a collection of small ghosts, young ghosts, but no less potent for their size and age.

A. N.

CONTENTS

ANCIENT EVILS

To disturb or awaken that which has its roots in the savage years of the past, when people walked a narrow path between vast lands of ever-dark, is one of the familiar touches of the ghost story. Modern men, women, and children are not armed against these ancient evils, and when they are forced to face them—then come pain, disaster, abiding ills.

SALOOZY

Margery Lawrence

(Note.—This is an early adventure of Dr. Miles Pennoyer, told by himself to his friend Jerome Latimer.)

WHEN I was a young man—which, I'm sorry to say, is quite a while ago!—I went down one summer to spend a couple of months with my young widowed sister, Clare Frant, at "Wichart's Farm," a small country house she had taken for herself, her two children—Michael, aged seven, and Susan, aged four—and Nannie, her faithful old maid, now turned nurse.

Clare had been widowed only a few months before Susan's birth—Naunton Frant, her husband and one of my best friends, had been lost with his ship somewhere in the China Seas almost eighteen months before this story opens. And in point of fact Clare's decision, as soon as his affairs were all tidied up, to move to Wichart's Farm, ultimately proved the luckiest of her life, as it was there she ran into Alan Hemingway, a brother of an old schoolmate and a first-class fellow, whom she married a few years later, a marriage that turned out extremely happily. But that is another story.

When I went down to stay with her she had only been at the farm a couple of months, and was still in the stage of settling down, getting acquainted with the countryside, the neighbours, the local village and its shops, and all the rest of it.

I was several years older than Clare (who was still only twenty-eight) and was very tired after spending eighteen months in Egypt undergoing a course of special training

3

there; so I was thankful to be back in England, and looked forward greatly to seeing Clare's new home, over which she had been positively lyrical in her letters. We were both country-born and -bred, so the prospect of a month or six weeks spent amongst the green fields and rustic byways that I loved was more than pleasant after the dust, heat, and smell of the East. So it was with a light heart that I set out from London one sunny day in June in my little Rover, arriving at Tanfield, the village nearest to Wichart's Farm, somewhere around six o'clock—but there I found myself bogged as to which way to turn.

I knew the farm lay some distance off, on the further side of the village, on a rather unfrequented side road. But that was all, and Clare's instructions as to how to find her new home had been vague in the extreme; so I pulled up at Tanfield's tiny Post Office, at the head of its single street, and dived in. There was a fat, apple-faced old body behind the little counter, which was piled with sweets, cigarettes, picture-postcards and various other oddments as well as telegram forms and postage stamps—she looked at me quickly and rather oddly, I thought, as I put my question, and said:

"You'll be Mrs. Frant's brother, I'm thinking, sir. Dr. Pennoyer—the gentleman she's expecting?"

I nodded, and she paused a moment, then came out from behind the little counter and gave me short and lucid directions as to how to find my way to the farm. I thanked her and was climbing back into my seat behind the wheel, when she said with a rather curious abruptness:

"She's a nice young lady, Mrs. Frant—and them children are right sweet little things, bless 'em. I hope everything's all right down there?"

I looked at her, faintly surprised.

"Dear me, I think so. I certainly hope so!" I said, amused. "What should go wrong? I haven't heard of any difficulties." The old lady looked at me uncertainly and her red-apple cheeks deepened in colour a trifle.

"Oh—I just asked," she said non-committally. "Sometimes a lady coming into a strange place finds things not everything she fancies . . . not that Mrs. Frant's the complaining sort. Indeed, she's as cheery as the day's long and ready to turn her hand to anything. I just wondered . . ." she hesitated and then evidently making up her mind she had said enough, finished her sentence on a different note. "Perhaps you'd tell her from me—Mrs. Pressing's the name, sir, of Tanfield Post Office—that there's some more of them peppermint humbugs come in that young Master Michael's so fond of, and I've taken the liberty of keeping some back for him? If I didn't they'd be all gone, maybe, before she comes down. And will you tell her too, sir, that . . . well, if anything should happen and she wants help, to telephone me at the Post Office and I'll be ready to do anything I can? She's not to hesitate? Thank you kindly, sir, and I wish you a very good afternoon."

She retreated hastily into her lair, as I opened my mouth on another question, and letting out the clutch I resumed my drive—and as I went I ruminated, thoughtful and faintly puzzled, on the little conversation, yet could make nothing of it. It was plain that Mrs. Pressing, worthy body, was somehow uneasy as to whether my sister was comfortable or not in her new home—but the sentence about "if she wanted help" had an odd and faintly sinister ring, and I did not quite like it. What should Clare want "help" over?

The house had been tested for sound drains, pipes, water supply, all the rest and passed OK, and though lack of domestic service was hitting the country as well as the town, Clare had told me she had managed to arrange for a daily girl to come in from the village, and with Nannie and her own capable hands, she was managing finely. What other difficulties were likely to crop up? My mind was still busy with the problem when I saw a break in the luxuriantly flowering hedge on my right, and a white gate standing ajar—I had arrived at Wichart's Farm, and Clare, looking pink and blooming and better than I had seen her for years, was running to meet me down the weedgrown drive from the white porch of a charming ivy-grown house that might have come straight out of a film set.

We hugged each other delightedly, and I parked the car in a dilapidated stable somewhere at the rear of the house—which had been originally, Clare told me later, the Dower House belonging to a once great mansion, now ruined and derelict. I lugged my suitcase out and we went arm-in-arm up to my room, a low-roofed little apartment with white-washed walls, a board floor innocent of rugs or carpet, and distinctly ramshackle furniture, as Clare had had to furnish her new abode with any oddments she could pick up cheaply at local sales or beg from her friends and relatives. She possessed very little furniture of her own, as up to poor Naunton's death her life, like that of most naval wives, had been spent in furnished lodgings in Portsmouth, Chatham, and similar places.

But if the room was bare and shabby, purple clematis and white-starred jasmine fringed the window frame; outside there was a cherry tree with great clusters of ruddy fruit shining between its glossy leaves, beyond the rambling wildness of the garden there were fields yellow with buttercups and studded with ruminating cows, and in the distance green hills rising against the blueness of the sky, so my spirits rose high as Clare helped me unpack my things, chattering like a monkey as she did so. Clare and I had lost our parents early, so we had grown up together more or less alone and were, I think, rather more to each other than are many brothers and sisters; and as she had made her move to the country in my absence I was all agog to know details.

Wichart's Farm had been the most amazing find—she struck it quite by chance, she told me, and couldn't believe her ears when she heard the low rental asked for it, thought there must be some catch somewhere! She had sent a friend, an expert in judging house property, down to spy out the land and find the "catch" before taking it; but he had found none, and advised her to jump at the chance at such a bargain—so she had taken it on a long lease and was delighted with it.

My things by this time unpacked, I had a wash in the bathroom at the far end of the passage—an amenity fortunately built in by a previous tenant—and proceeded to accompany my sister on a tour of the house; it still lacked half an hour to dinner-time, which she took early on account of the children, and at the moment, in the large sunny kitchen in lieu of the dining-room that was, some time in the near future, to be properly equipped.

I found the house considerably larger than I had antici- pated, though Clare had described it as a "country cottage" and had certainly got it at a cottage rental—and it was sound and substantial enough, though badly in need of repairs, painting and papering and so on, which I privately resolved to have done at my own expense as soon as possible.

Clare's own bedroom I had peeped into on my way down- stairs, and found it a larger edition of my own, but rather better furnished. Beyond Clare's room there was a third, rather larger room that was the night-nursery, where Nannie and the children slept; and across the narrow corridor were several deep cupboards and two more small rooms. At the moment these two were crowded with trunks, odd bits of unsorted furniture, cardboard boxes, newspapers, and similar junk—but one would become a bedroom for Nannie in time, when sufficient furnishings could be collected; the second a room for Michael, when he reached an age and dignity that necessitated one.

On the ground floor, besides the kitchen and scullery, there were only three rooms. One small one leading off the kitchen—this Clare told me she meant some time to turn into a sewing-cum-sitting-room for herself and Nannie; another small one facing the front that would ultimately make a very nice little dining-room, and one large central lounge—origi- nally two rooms, one at the front and another at the back of the house, that had been knocked into one. The result was a really handsome lounge with two windows, one at each end; one ordinary small one facing the drive and another at the back, this a double french window or pair of glass doors that led directly out upon the garden . . . where, Clare firmly informed me, any amount of work awaited my doing directly I should feel energetic enough to undertake it!

On this room Clare had concentrated her main furnishing

efforts up to date. She had sent a frantic SOS to all her relatives and friends to spare her what they could, and the results
were both charming and homelike. The floor had been
stained and polished—though the stain hadn't come off her
hands for days, my sister ruefully said—there was a worn but
colourful Indian rug before the deep red-brick fireplace and
another before the french window; a low embroidered fire-
seat that I remembered as belonging to an aged aunt of ours,
and a sofa and two easy chairs covered with faded but pretty
cretonne in delphinium blues and mauves, on a cream
ground . . . these Clare had picked up cheaply, she said, at a
local sale There was a little oak gateleg table and one or two
odd chairs from various cousins, a set of bookshelves from an
old admirer, a mirror in an old gilt frame from another, and
an Italian "sunray" wall clock from a third—did I mention
that my sister was very pretty?—and with a set of coffee-
coloured "lustre" jugs gleaming on the mantelpiece and the
windows draped with blue and cream striped linen curtains,
it was a room that would have done credit to anybody, let
alone a hard-up young naval officer's widow. And so I told
Clare as I poured her out a glass of her own sherry—a dozen
of that delectable *apéritif* having been contributed as their
"share" towards Clare's new venture by three young naval
lads who had served with Naunton some years earlier.

Clare flushed with gratification—flushed almost as pink as
her pretty cotton frock—and slipping a hand through my
arm, squeezed it affectionately.

"Bless you! I'm *so* glad you like it," she said. "I hoped you
would. Now you've got to forget magic and mysteries and all
the other weirds you're studying and loaf with me! I'm going
to adore having you all to myself for at least a month, I hope,
to help me weed and prune and dig and generally get the
garden into shape. I'm going to have this place looking a
picture sooner or later, and I think I'm going to be very
happy here once I'm well settled in."

"Lucky we were both brought up in the country, so you
don't mind loneliness," I said. Clare opened her eyes wide.

"Lonely? I'm too busy to think much about being lonely!"

she said. "But anyway, I'm sure I shall have as many friends as I want very soon. I've met the Vicar and his wife and one or two others, and I've just discovered that Sybil Hemingway— d'you remember her, she was at Miss Crabbe's with me?—is married and living down here. She's Lady Curtis, of the Hall—imagine Sybil Lady Curtis!—we ran into each other at the Post Office in Tanfield only the other day, and she was simply delighted to see me and has promised to introduce everybody nice in the neighbourhood."

"That reminds me," I said, and proceeded to deliver old Mrs. Pressing's message, at which Clare raised her eyebrows.

"That's nice of the old soul," she commented. "But I don't quite see why I should send out any SOS. Of course I'm having the usual minor troubles consequent on coming into a house that's been uninhabited for a good many years—an occasional leak or gutters stopped up, mice and cockroaches all over the place, and so on—but I'm coping with them quite adequately. As you say, there's something in being country-bred, one takes this sort of thing in one's stride. But it's rather odd . . . Sybil Curtis said something of the same sort to me when she said goodbye the other day . . . something about my getting in touch with her immediately if I needed help." She brooded. "Funny! I wonder what . . ."

"Oh, I expect it's only an excess of neighbourly feeling," I said breezily. "Anyway it's good to know that you've got nice friendly people round you ready to rush to the rescue if you need 'em!" I looked round the room again appreciatively. "Really delightful room this is, Clare—but almost painfully tidy. I remember your quarters in Chatham always littered with toys and things for the kids . . ."

"Thank heaven I've got room enough here for them to have a proper playroom," said Clare. "Nice days, of course, they are always out in the garden, but when it's wet or chilly there's a huge empty attic on the top floor—the one above the bedrooms—that they use. Though sometimes I hope to be able to make a playroom out of the big loft above the old stable that you're using as a garage now. I'd like that better."

"Why?" I asked curiously. "If there's a good-sized room

already for them *in* the house, I can't see the sense of throwing away money on making another room *outside* the house!"

Clare frowned.

"I can't say *why*," she admitted, "and it sounds mad—but
somehow I don't altogether *like* that attic!"

"What's it like?" I demanded.

"Well," said my sister, "it's certainly a fine big place. It's
practically the whole top floor. It's light and sunny enough,
and certainly it's dry and there's heaps of room, and the
children love it, especially Mike—and yet, *somehow* I don't
like it!"

"You should worry?" I said. "If the kids can't fall out of
the window . . ." Clare shook her head, "and there aren't
any fires for them to fall into, or ladders for them to fall
down, I should think you'd be thankful for such a place to
park them in while Nannie can get on with her work in the
house."

"I know," nodded Clare. "But still . . ." She broke off her
sentence as Nannie poked her head round the door and
greeted me with a broad smile of welcome.

"Dinner's ready, m'am—and I'm glad to see you, sir!" she
said all in one breath. "And could you come in at once,
m'am, because it's hot, and Baby's at the table and I don't
like to leave her?" She vanished as we drank up the last of
our drinks and moved towards the door.

"Thank goodness Nannie's cooked the dinner," said Clare
contentedly. "We take it in turns as a rule, and I look forward to my evenings off. I *do* like dinner cooked for me, so
that I can change and rest a bit and feel fresh for the
evening."

"I thought you'd got a girl from the village working for
you?" I said. "Can't she cook dinner for you?" Clare frowned.

"Well," she said, "she's not a bad cook, Ada, and she does
the lunches, but the bore is she *won't* stay after seven o'clock
—and I really can't eat before seven-thirty, it makes such a
dreary long evening. Even that's late to have Baby up, I
know, but I really can't help it. This girl only lives just down
the road, yet she insists on leaving at seven—won't stay a

minute longer." I nodded—it was not until some time later on that the significance of this reluctance to stay late on the part of young Ada Price dawned on me, and by that time I had learned that her dislike of Wichart's Farm after dark extended to the entire village! But naturally at the moment it didn't strike me as at all unusual, though inconvenient for my sister, and we sat down to dinner.

The kitchen was a pleasant, old-fashioned place with a red tiled floor, an immense black kitchen range beside which the small modern gas stove used by Clare and Nannie looked an impertinent anachronism, and a large built-in dresser crowded with vari-coloured plates and dishes; it had huge black beams overhead that still retained the iron hooks from which in earlier, more opulent days had swung hams and bacon, strings of onions, dried herbs, apple-rings, and other luscious things, and in the middle was a square table spread with a blue and white checkered cloth, at which the baby Susan was already sitting in her high chair, her bib ruffled up to her ears, her fair hair on end, beating the table hungrily with her spoon. I received from her a wet and sticky kiss and a coy smile—I was one of young Susan's favourites; she was already, at barely four years, distinctly choosey in her boy friends!—and Nannie was just placing a large brown casserole upon the table from whence was issuing a more than tempting savour, when Clare spoke.

"Why Nannie, where's Michael? Still in the garden?"

Nannie flushed a trifle and all but tossed her head as she turned to get the hot plates.

"I brought Master Michael in from the garden in plenty of time for his dinner, ma'am—he was all washed and ready two minutes ago. And I'd only just put Baby in her chair when he was out again and off! Down to that tree he's so fond of—playing, I'll bet, with that Saloozy! I called after him, but it wasn't no use—he was off like a streak, the naughty boy, and I suppose now I'll have to go and fetch him in and wash him all over again!"

She dumped a pair of vegetable dishes and a heaped salad-bowl before us and departed, via the far door, out into the

garden, and we could hear her vexed voice calling as she
went.

"Master Mike—Master Michael! Now you're late for dinner, and your uncle's come, and why *must* you be such a
naughty boy . . ."

I looked at my sister.

" 'Saloozy'? What on earth's she talking about?"

Clare's smooth brow was creased by a faintly puzzled frown
as she helped the stewed rabbit, shaking her head as I refused
the meat—you know my vegetarian principles—but accepted
the fresh green salad, delicious country peas, and baked
potatoes.

"I honestly don't know," she said. "Look here, Miles,
would you ever have called Mike a specially imaginative
child—more than any other normal child, I mean?" I shook
my head and she went on thoughtfully. "Well, I can't say I'm
worried exactly—but I'm puzzled that ever since we came to
live here Mike keeps on talking about somebody he calls
'Saloozy' in *the* most peculiar way."

" 'Saloozy'—sounds like an extension of Susan," I said with
my mouth full. "Does he mean Susan? If not, perhaps there's
some small local child he plays with that he calls that."

"Sue's always called 'Baby'—and anyway I asked him that,
and he said no, that Saloozy was a 'he,' " said Clare. "And
there *aren't* any children living at all near. The only children
handy are the Vicar's boy and girl, who are a good deal older
than Mike, twelve and thirteen, I think, or something like
that, and not in the least likely to come in voluntarily and
play with a little boy like Mike."

I pondered, munching salad, while Clare spooned gravy
over Susan's potatoes and rescued her rag doll from being
plunged head foremost into the resultant savoury mess.

"I'm not an authority on children," I said at last. "But I
believe a good many kids invent some sort of an invisible
playmate, don't they? Sounds like something of that sort . . .
after all, Susan's rather young to make a companion for
Mike."

"I know," said Clare. "But surely the sort of child that invents invisible playmates is rather the—imaginative, dreamy sort of child? Whereas Mike's just a nice, normal, ordinary little boy."

He certainly looked normal enough just then as he was more or less dragged into the room by Nannie, his ears red with washing, his small face rebellious—he had been scrubbed afresh in the scullery sink before being allowed to come to table. But as he saw me sitting grinning at him he forgot his temper, rushed at me and hugged me like a small bear, clamouring a dozen questions, and when these were satisfied he climbed into his seat and fell upon his plate of stew with an appetite that certainly had nothing abnormal about it.

"Mike!" Clare's voice was reproachful. "You shouldn't have been late for dinner, you know—Nannie had washed you and got you ready, and you *knew* Uncle Miles was coming."

Michael paused in his eating and looked sideways at his mother—a look partly guilty, partly repentant, and faintly defiant all at the same time.

"I know, Mummy—I'm sorry. But I tried to 'splain to Nannie. I *had* to go. I had to put somethin' back I'd been playing with."

"Now Master Michael!" Nannie's voice was severe as she changed the plates and placed stewed cherries and creamed rice on the table. "You *know* that isn't true! When we came in from the garden to get ready for dinner you helped me carry *all* your toys in, and there wasn't a thing left outside! You only had your little horse and your bat and ball, and Baby her three dollies and some picture books anyway . . . how can you tell such a story?"

The small boy bent over his plate. His ears were suffused with a sullen flush but his lips were set stubbornly.

"It wasn't a story!" he muttered. Clare looked at him uncertainly.

"But Mike, *darling*," she said. "If everything was brought in from the garden, as Nannie says, how *can* you have gone back to put anything away? You must be telling a fib for some reason—and you know mother hates her little boy to tell fibs."

Michael looked at her appealingly.

"But Mummy," he began. "It wasn't . . . wasn't anything *ordinary*—I mean like my horse or any sort of toy. I . . . *had* to put it back. It wasn't mine. It was only lent to me."

By this time I was getting interested.

"What was it, Mike?" I said. "And who did it belong to?" The child hesitated a moment, glanced round the table as though sizing up the atmosphere, and then spoke half-defiantly.

"It was a stick. It was Saloozy's stick. I'd been playing with Saloozy."

"You see," said Clare, as we sat in the lounge discussing things later on that evening over our cigarettes, "that's how it goes . . . and Miles, I really don't know how to handle it! It's futile to take up Nannie's attitude and punish or lecture him for telling lies—that's the old-fashioned method, and I don't agree with it. I thought at first, as you did, that it was some sort of game he was playing with Susan, but I soon found it wasn't that. He wanders off by himself these days to play alone—which seems to mean playing, or *pretending* he's playing at least, with somebody called 'Saloozy,' of all absurd names! He never *used* to be a fanciful sort of child—it's only since he came here, and I can't make it out." She frowned at her cigarette. "I'm rather afraid I took up the wrong attitude in the beginning—I tried to laugh him out of it, and now I wish I hadn't. He's sort of retreated into himself and evades talking about it now, unless he's driven into a corner—and then he says as little as he can, but persists in saying he is telling the truth." She frowned. "I really can't make it out—and I refuse to believe that my jolly, ordinary, healthy little Mike is a potential medium, seeing and talking to a ghost-child!"

"Who and what *is* Saloozy, anyway?" I asked. Clare shook her head.

"I don't know. All he says is that he's just 'Saloozy' and that he plays with him. He says he won't come if anybody else is there, and that it doesn't happen every day, but quite often . . . and I don't know whether it's my imagination, but it seems to be happening more and more often this last week or two."

"Odd freak of the imagination," I said. "Doesn't seem like the kid as I remember him!"

My sister shook her head. "No! Mike's altered in a good many ways lately and I can't make it out. He's grown much quieter and more bookish—he never used to want to read, but now he closets himself for hours at a time with books, spelling out words that are too long for him and looking *so* absorbed. And he's absent-minded, and doesn't touch the toys he used to play with, except an old round pocket mirror he found somewhere—and what he wants with that I can't think, but he persists in carrying it about with him. Also he's not half as reliable as he used to be. When we came here first I used to be able to leave him to look after Baby in the garden while Nannie helped me in the house—he was quite proud of the responsibility and mounted guard over her in the most amusing way. But now he wanders off—generally down to an old ash tree, the tree Nannie spoke of, he seems to like playing there better than anywhere else in the garden—and leaves Baby alone. And it isn't *like* Mike to leave a job he's been asked to do! I can't make it out at all." She sighed. "Well, children are queer little cusses and I suppose it's simply some sort of a phase he's passing through. Shall we go to bed? And tomorrow if you feel strong enough we might try a little tidying up of the garden."

A peaceful week passed, luckily with lovely weather, and during that week Clare and I had really begun to make a difference to the wildly overgrown garden and orchard. It was a sizeable garden and had endless possibilities, and as we worked Clare talked of keeping hens and rabbits and growing vegetables and fruit and flowers for the market, as though in her small energetic person she combined the strength of five men, all of which she would certainly have needed to carry

out her full programme! I made up my mind to tell her
before I left that I would stand the wages of a full-time
gardener, which would be a great help to her—she could only
afford, on her income, to pay Nannie and her "daily," the
local wench who was so anxious to get away home at seven.

In Clare's company I explored the place thoroughly, assuring her, to her delight, that she could put in hand as soon as
she liked the repairing, painting, and papering of the house,
from the old-fashioned cellars to the attics—or rather the
single attic, the room the children used as a wet-day playroom. This last place interested me considerably, though I
had been at the farm some days before I exerted myself
sufficiently to climb the stairs to the top floor. Clare had
assured me that there was nothing to see—it was just an
empty oblong attic—but somehow I was vaguely curious
about the place, especially as Clare had said she "disliked" it.

I wondered, as I mounted the steep old stairs, dusty,
uncarpeted, and pitted with cracks and mouseholes here and
there, what odd bee she had got in her bonnet—it was not like
Clare to "take fancies," as Nannie would have said.

At the top of the attic flight a short narrow passage
stretched before me, with a deep cupboard lined with shelves
set into the wall on one side, and on the other, a door set ajar
that gave onto a small shallow closet of some sort. The end of
the passage was blocked by another door—obviously this
passage was all that was left of an old corridor that had once
run down the centre of the top floor, dividing it into front
rooms and back. I walked down the passage, pushed open the
door and found myself in the famous attic—a long shooting-
gallery of a room that occupied the entire top storey.

My first impression was—curiously—one of gloom, although
my second, astonished, told me that this was nonsense. The
long room, with its sloping black roof-beams, peeling walls,
and uneven wooden floor, was actually sunny enough . . .
indeed it was full of sunlight, thanks to the dormer windows,
four on the front, three at the back, that let in light on both
sides of its echoing length; and later on I realised that my

impression of gloom was purely a psychic one—and well deserved!

It was quite empty, and seemed half-asleep and blinking in the dusty sunlight that slanted in through the small hooded windows—yet as I stood there surveying the room, I knew what Clare had meant when she talked about disliking it. Instantly—and quite irrationally—I knew that I also disliked it! Startled and curious, I stood still a moment, wondering at my own sensations, and staring down the room . . . it was plain, as Clare had said, that the walls of the passage and those of the small rooms on each side of it had been pulled down so as to turn the entire top floor, except the very short section at the top of the stairs, into one large room. Not only did the walls, roof-beams, and floor show traces of brickwork having been removed, but sections of the wall, right and left, showed remains of several different wallpapers, and I scratched my head, puzzled. I could see the sense of throwing two ground-floor rooms into one to make a good-sized lounge—but why spoil the attics? I should have thought, regarding the top storey, that several small rooms for use as spare rooms, servants' quarters, or for storage purposes would have been vastly more convenient than the one immensely long low-roofed chamber. I walked thoughtfully round the walls, and noted that at the far end there had been a fire-place—quite a large, deep fireplace too, and well-used, if the blackened brickwork round the opening meant anything. And close beside it, from one side of the wall projected several odd pieces of rusted ironwork, broken off as though something that had once been built in there had been roughly torn away. . . .

The chimney-breast where the fireplace was situated projected slightly into the room, and above the fireplace ran a shallow mantelshelf of brickwork. Above this was fixed to the wall an old carved and gilded frame containing a coloured print—much faded, and torn in one or two places—of a typical "Christmas Annual" painting of a small child, white-frilled and blue-ribboned, playing with a large St. Bernard dog. I walked up to examine it, wondering why such an inanity should have been thought worthy of a handsome old frame, when a small voice spoke behind me.

"Saloozy lives in here!"

I turned round, startled, to see Michael, whom I had only just left playing in the garden with the new scooter I had brought down from London for him as a present.

"What on earth brings you up here?" I demanded.

"Oh, I knew!" said the boy. "I knew you'd come up here. I always know when anybody comes into Saloozy's room. He tells me."

I stared at the child, suspicious, sceptical, yet oddly impressed. Standing there in the dusty slanting sunlight, in his crumpled blue cotton suit, with his rough fair hair on end, Michael was so obviously, as Clare had said, a jolly, ordinary little boy, that this hint of the uncanny, the inexplicable about him struck a most odd and alien note . . . and yet a note that one could not quite ignore. Whoever 'Saloozy' was—or was not—it was plain that he was very real to this child. . . .

There was a low seat built into the brickwork of the wall below each window, and sitting down on the nearest, I drew Michael to me. He came readily enough, and I wondered whether possibly I might, as somebody completely new, who had not yet thrown either doubt or derision upon his illusion, find out something definite about it.

"How do you mean 'tells' you, Mike?" I began. "And anyway—who *is* he?"

"I don't know how he tells me," said the child frankly. "But . . . I just know. And he's—well, he's Saloozy. That's all I know. And he *is* real! I don't care what Nannie and Mummy say!" His small face was obstinate, and I hastened to agree.

"I'm sure he is, Mike, if you say so. But can't you tell me any more about him?" An oddly cunning look crept into the childish face at my knee and he shook his head.

"He doesn't like being talked about," he said briefly. "He's just Saloozy, and he lives here and he's showing me how to do things . . . oh, wonderful things!" His blue eyes suddenly blazed, bright, amazed. "You can't *think* what splendid things . . . and he's going to teach me lots more. Only . . ." his face clouded over. "He says I got to work hard and learn things at school so as to make it easier . . ." He looked up at my face anxiously. "Uncle Miles, is it very hard to learn Latin?"

"Latin?" I stared, frankly confounded, and he nodded sagely and went on:

"Can't start training too early, Saloozy says. And Latin's terribly 'portant in learning about—about . . ." his voice sank oddly to an almost awed whisper, "about *Them* and how to make *Them* do what you want. There's books and books I got to read some day. Books in Latin an' Greek too, and specially the Big Book, when I know enough . . . and he wants me to start soon."

"But what *for?*" I asked incredulously. "And who are They? Are—er—They part of Saloozy's idea too?"

He evaded a direct answer but repeated his question—was it hard to learn Latin?—and when I pressed him further he slipped out of my arms and said he was hungry, he wanted his tea, couldn't we go down? There was plainly no more to be got out of him then; so I dropped the matter, told him that if he really wanted to try to learn Latin I would start him on the rudiments right away—needless to say, in my studies a pretty thorough knowledge of Greek and Latin is essential— upon which he threw his arms round me and hugged me ecstatically, and we went downstairs together.

I said nothing about the little encounter to Clare, as I didn't want to worry her—and though I stubbornly told myself there was nothing to worry over, "Saloozy" was simply an imaginary playmate that the boy had invented, yet I found myself oddly uneasy whenever I thought about it, as I did a good many times during the ensuing days. Clare was puzzled, I could see, but rather gratified when I told her I was going to start Michael in Latin, and I was astonished to see how quickly he seemed to grasp it, as he had not shown any marked ability or even interest in his lessons up to date.

Now he was patently eager to learn—certainly, I told myself, Clare was right when she said that Michael had changed a good deal. Besides spending a great deal of time in reading any and everything he could lay hands on, especially old tales of fairy lore, magic, legend and that sort of thing, from being a rather noisy, romping, slap-dash little boy he had grown markedly quiet, and showed a tendency to "sneak about and come up behind a body without making a sound," so Nannie vexedly averred. Also he now patently preferred his own company to that of others, and scarcely ever looked at the toys or games he used to love—things like lead soldiers, his airgun, bricks, Meccano, and similar things usually dear to a small boy's heart now lay about unnoticed. How he amused himself now nobody seemed to know. When asked he merely said vaguely, "Oh, just messing about"; and by chance one day I came across him engaged in one form of "messing about" which was certainly a curious amusement for a little boy of seven to choose!

I was planting beansticks for some late-sown scarlet runners in the now largely cleared and weeded kitchen garden when I saw Michael and Nannie emerging from the back door of the kitchen. Nannie's face was scarlet with annoyance, Michael wriggling and squirming furiously as she held him firmly by the shoulder; and in her spare hand Nannie was gingerly carrying a little enamel saucepan. Catching sight of me she hailed me instantly.

"Oh, Mr. Miles, sir, where's madam? She *must* do something with this naughty boy! This is the third time I've caught him trying to boil up some nasty weeds on my stove— to get the juice, he says. Using my saucepan to do it in too, and I might have used it for Baby's milk after and poisoned her, poor child!" She looked down at Michael and shook him angrily. "You bad wicked boy! If ever I catch you doing such a thing again . . ."

"That's all right, Nannie," I said. "I'll take charge of Master Michael—I'm sure he didn't mean any harm. It isn't worth worrying madam over. Give me the saucepan. You run back to the kitchen and leave him to me."

Nannie looked doubtful, but released her captive and went into the house—and I looked curiously at Michael. He was looking after her, and the expression on his small face was so venomous that I was quite startled. He had always been a singularly sweet-tempered little boy, and I decided that children were evidently capable of stronger feeling than I had imagined as I poked a finger into the seaweed-like green mess in the saucepan.

"What *is* all this, Mike?" I said. "Go on, you can tell me—I won't be cross. What on earth were you trying to do with this green stuff, and what is it?"

He frowned, hesitated, and answered brusquely.

"It's . . . several things. I don't know their names. But Saloozy shows me what to pick. He wants me to try and learn to dis . . . dis . . . ."

"Do you mean distilling?" I asked, amazed. Michael nodded eagerly.

"Oh yes—that's the word. I don't know how, but he was going to show me . . . only it's so *difficult*! I know there ought to be a special room to do it in . . . I can't remember, but I've seen it *somewhere*. I know! A long time ago . . . somewhere where there's a fire, that always had to be kept going with some old leather bellows that were awful heavy to blow, or *he* would get dreadfully cross. And there's a long sort of table with lots of funny glass things, tubes and bottles and pots . . . only they're not called that, somehow. I can't remember what they *are* called. Wait! Al—alumpics and . . . and 'torts an' matesses and cocoabits and . . . and a lot of other things. Saloozy used to be there dis . . . dis . . . what you said—making coloured juices out of flowers and plants and things, and he used to laugh and say,

> 'Some to cure and some to kill
> Some to make your brainbox ill.
> Some to bend you to my will . . .' "

He stopped, and I had an odd impression that he had *been* stopped, not stopped of his own accord . . . and suddenly, quite unaccountably, I felt a faint prickling as the hairs rose along the back of my neck! There, standing in the kitchen garden, in the serene rays of the afternoon sun, I felt the first real hint of "queerness" behind all this talk of Saloozy . . . a queerness that was not of this normal earth.

"Look here, old man," I said gently. "This friend of yours—this Saloozy—interests me very much. We talked about him the other day—don't you remember? Can't you tell me more about him?"

He slanted an oddly cunning look at me and shook his head.

"I can't," he said briefly. "I told you, he doesn't like being talked about . . . he says I talk too much as it is. He wants me not to waste time talking, but to listen and learn! And I *am* trying . . . I was trying to learn with this." He looked gloomily at the enamel saucepan.

"Well, experimenting by boiling odd weed in kitchen pots and pans that are used for cooking food in is dangerous, and you certainly mustn't do *that* again," I said decidedly. "If you want to, later on you can take up chemistry—which will teach you about such things as distilling essences and so on. Though what on earth's got into a small boy like you—only seven—to want to study things like Latin and chemistry I can't imagine, Mike! You aren't putting on some sort of an act, are you?" He said nothing, only compressed his lips and looked obstinate, and I gave it up—no use antagonising the child. I should get nothing out of him that way. I handed him over the saucepan.

"Now run along and wash that out nicely and give it back to Nannie, and say you're sorry for dirtying up her things."

He hesitated, taking the pan reluctantly.

"I don't like Nannie," he muttered. "She hurt my shoul-der—she scolds me. I'd like to teach her . . ."

I looked at him, astonished. Mike and Nannie, in the old days had been the best of friends, and it was not like the sunny, good-natured little boy I knew to bear malice for a scolding or a shaking.

"Don't be silly, Mike," I said. "Forget it—and run and do as I said."

He turned on his heel without a word and went into the house, and I went back to my beansticks, pondering as I worked. I was distinctly disturbed. From whence had young Michael, aged seven, got his vivid mental picture of a medieval alchemist's laboratory?

"A fire always hot, that someone blew with bellows—never allowed to go out—a long table with funny-shaped glass things," and the obvious attempt to recall the words "alembic," "retort," "cucurbit," and above all, the old word *matrass*—now called flask—that I would take my oath he could not possibly have come across, even in his sudden interest in reading? I was likewise doubtful if he had ever seen a pair of bellows—what modern child has, unless they happen to have lived in some remote country place where such a thing is still used? Michael's young life had been spent in seaside lodgings, and his notion of fire was a gas stove!

I was sufficiently interested, later on that night, to leaf through all the children's books Clare possessed, but found nothing beyond the usual classical fairy tales, Grimm, Hans Andersen, *Arabian Nights,* and so on, scattered among old volumes of *Little Folks, Our Darlings, Peter Rabbit, Chistopher Robin,* and so on. There was nothing in any of them that could possibly have suggested such a scene to a small boy's mind. I was more puzzled than ever, but again said nothing to Clare. And on the following day I was lying still ruminating on it in the hammock that I had with Clare's help just slung between two stout trees outside the lounge windows, when I spied Michael stealing cautiously down the path beyond a belt of syringa bushes that led to his favourite corner of the garden, a sort of dell that was shaded by a fine old ash tree.

He plainly did not want me to see him, and I don't know by what impulse I suddenly slipped out of the hammock and followed him—luckily I had by this time cleared the garden paths, cut back the undergrowth and done a good deal of

tidying-up in general, so could walk after him without trip-
ping and blundering over sprawling outgrowths. I saw him
dive into a shallow little hollow at the foot of the ash tree,
and pausing behind a towering laurel bush that adequately
screened me from his view, I watched him curiously. He was,
as far as I could see, rigging up a queer little arrangement of
two sticks with a long bit of string between them—thrusting
the sticks into the earth at such a distance from each other
that the string was drawn taut, as a washing-line is drawn.
And as I watched he proceeded to pin to the string several
odd scraps such as two or three dropped green leaves, a
couple of bits of paper, a twig, a corner torn from his
handkerchief, precisely as pieces of washing are strung along
a line.

I stared, interested and curious, as the row of fragments
being fixed to his satisfaction to the line of string, Michael sat
back, surveyed the arrangement, then fumbled amongst the
roots of the tree and brought out what looked to me like a
small dark stick of wood. Rising to his feet, he stood stock still
for a moment, holding the stick directly over the line of
string, stretched between its miniature wooden props. His
small face was flushed, intent, and I could see that his lips
were moving, though I was not near enough to hear what he
was saying—and suddenly I felt a return of that queer and
unpleasant sense of *grue* that had overtaken me in the garden
the day before! It was a baking hot day, almost oppressive, yet
a sensation as of icy water being poured down my spine seized
me as I stood and stared—and lo and behold, without his
touching it at all as far as I could see, the miniature washing-
line crumpled, staggered, and fell to the ground . . . and
from somewhere behind me I could hear Clare's light pretty
voice calling.

"Miles, Miles! Here's Sybil come over to tea and she's
brought her brother. Come and meet him."

We had a merry tea party, though after the fashion of
women Clare was fussed because she had had no notice and so
had not prepared any special cakes or sandwiches or things
like that. But there was fresh crusty bread and good country

butter from the farm down the lane, and a pot of honey and another of recently made red cherry jam, and lettuces and radishes. Sybil had brought with her a basket of the strawberries for which the Hall was famous, which we ate with lashings of cream, and I said—and Sybil agreed—that anybody who wanted a better tea than that didn't deserve to get any tea at all. Sybil's brother was a nice shy sort of chap of about thirty-eight or so, who had just been invalided out of the Army minus a leg, and was planning to come and live somewhere near his sister. I liked him on sight, and he plainly liked me and more than liked Clare, who was looking her prettiest in a new yellow linen frock that by sheer Providence—or so she assured me afterwards—she had just put on to see how it looked; and that meeting led to much, as I have already indicated.

Alan Hemingway was still too unused to his artificial leg to risk much moving about, so after tea Sybil and I left him comfortably planted in a lounge chair chatting to Clare while I went round the garden with Sybil, to show her—not without a certain amount of justifiable pride—the great improvement that Clare and I had effected since my arrival a fortnight earlier.

I had forgotten Sybil Hemingway, ungallant as it sounds, I know, until I met her again, and then I remembered her . . . a sturdy red-haired little girl with a deep voice, a snub nose, and lots of freckles, who could (to my boyish chagrin) bowl a far faster and straighter ball than I could ever do. She had altered very little—developed into a pleasant-looking, cheery woman of the traditional English country type. Wore tweeds and brogues superbly and probably looked hopeless in evening dress, went about hatless winter and summer, never moved without a stick and a couple of cocker spaniels at her heels; bullied the parson and the villagers, who all adored her, ruled her husband, her children and her domain in general with a kindly but iron hand, and won the local cup for flowers and vegetables grown at the Hall with almost monotonous regularity.

She was enthusiastic about the vastly improved appearance

of the garden, though she admitted she had never actually been inside it, only looked at it from the outside as she drove past into Tanfield . . . the sleepy lane in which Wichart's Farm was situated was a short cut from the Hall into the village, and she occasionally used it to save time. Though never, she added with her brusque laugh, when her Nannie was in the car . . . I looked at her sharply and she caught herself up, but it was too late.

"Whatever do you mean, Sybil?" I asked. She paused a moment, then shrugged her shoulders.

"Sorry . . . that slipped out. Don't tell Clare, I don't want to upset her, and its plain she hasn't been . . . upset . . . since she came, Lord forbid that I should start anything with her! But the fact is, Miles, local people—and my Nannie's a local girl—don't like this place, and avoid it as much as possible. And . . ." she paused a moment then plunged bluntly on, "to be absolutely honest, if I'd known Clare was thinking of taking the house—which I didn't until she was actually in it, and then it was too late—I'd have done my best to put her off it myself. So there!"

"No!" I stared at her, yet even as I stared I knew that to pretend surprise would be . . . just plain pretence. There *was* something odd about the Farm . . . I knew it. I had known it subconsciously ever since the moment I had walked into the Long Attic—and possibly before that, only I had not stopped to analyse my inner feelings. I pulled myself together. "Look here, Sybil, I'll be frank. I don't like admitting it . . . but several things have happened . . . *are* happening as far as that goes . . . here, that have set me thinking, and I want to try and get a fair slant on it. I won't tell Clare. Tell me what you know."

Sybil shook her head, frowning.

"Sorry, Miles, but there's so little I can tell! All I know is that this place simply doesn't seem lucky in its letting. People pounce on it and settle in, and then, very soon, on one excuse or another they clear out—no reason given—and it's empty again. It's as though there were *something*—some

'influence' I suppose the Spiritualists would call it—that pre-
vents anybody settling down there." She paused. "I'm sorry I
can't give you more details, but there it is."

"Aren't there any village stories going about?" I asked
disappointedly. "Though they may be exaggerated, still
sometimes they're useful on the no-smoke-without-fire prin-
ciple."

Sybil shook her head again.

"Well, I've heard nothing *definite*," she said. "The place
has simply vaguely got a bad name—you can't get a maid to
sleep there, or even stay after dusk. As regards village talk
in general—well, I'm not a native here, nor is Charlie; he
only inherited the Hall and the title quite unexpectedly.
We'd lived abroad for years before that and never seen this
place at all, actually. If we'd been born and bred here we'd
have soaked up the local traditions as we grew! But though
they like us well enough, we're still 'foreigners,' if you know
what I mean; and village folk are awfully shy and secretive
about discussing things like that with newcomers. I tried to
pump some of 'em about it when I came here first, but they
merely evade any direct reply—I've no doubt there *are* stories,
but I can't get at 'em. They probably talk plenty amongst
themselves, but they won't talk to us!"

"Know anything about the past history of the place?" I
asked.

"I'll ask Charlie," said Sybil. "But all I know is probably
what Clare knows herself—that Wichart's Farm is all that's
left of an old estate. The Farm is the Dower House—the big
house was burnt down several hundred years ago; it was
never rebuilt. You can still see the ruins in the wood, half a
mile away. The story goes that there was a curse on it—but
again, I don't know the details."

"Blow!" I said. "I hoped you'd be able to put me onto
something—there *is* something queer about the place, and
I'm convinced it centres in the Long Attic, whatever it is.
And there's another thing . . ." I paused. I did not want to
mention Michael and "Saloozy," and yet in my bones I knew

there was a connection. Had not Michael said, "Saloozy lives here"?

"Do tell me," began Sybil greedily, but I shook my head.

"Not until I've cleared it up—and then I'll tell you anything you like. But discussing a thing gives it added life and strength, you know, so we won't talk any more about it just now. I'll find a way of dealing with the thing somehow—but it *would* have been a help if you could have given me a line on it."

"I'll ask Charlie, to make sure, if he's come across anything, and get him to write you," said Sybil. "The Long Attic, you say—? Queer, Clare can't bear that room, she told me, and it's never used."

We both turned and looked back at the house, looking blandly picturesque, with its peaked gables and sloping roof mantled at one end by high-climbing clematis and pink rambler roses that made a cascade of foaming colour and scent almost from roof to ground . . . the four little dormer windows in the topmost storey seemed to watch us like hooded eyes, and Sybil gave an exclamation of surprise.

"Why, there's Michael! Look, up in that very attic, and he seems to be talking to somebody."

She was right!

There was Michael, sitting on the sill of one of the windows, plainly talking to somebody within the room—though from where we were standing it was impossible to see who it was. The child was patently explaining or describing something, his small hands waving, his head bobbing with excitement, and as we looked he brought both hands down upon his knees as though in an ecstasy of amusement and burst into shrill laughter . . . the window was open and we could hear his laughter ringing faintly on the warm still air. Then he turned, saw us looking up at the window, and immediately slipped away—and we looked at each other uncertainly.

"That's odd—just as we were talking about him," said Sybil slowly. "What should Mike be doing in an empty room?"

"Oh, Nannie or the girl might be up there for some reason and he's followed them," I said, more casually than I felt, as we turned to walk back to the house. "Clare says the children use the attic as a playroom sometimes. And Mike in particular has a positive yen for the place."

Sybil looked doubtful.

"Well," she said, "if I felt the way Clare feels about that room I don't think I'd be very keen for my children to use it! But still, it's probably all imagination, and certainly it sounds useful as a playroom, as you say. Ah, here we are! Come on, Alan, if you've done flirting with Clare. We must be getting home . . . after Clare's fixed a date to come over and see us?"

The date for our return visit having been fixed, we waved our visitors goodbye, and the sound of the car drawing away down the sunny, dusty road had only just died when Nannie, her round red face mottled with tears—most surprisingly, for she was a cheerful soul—poked her head round the door and beckoned to Clare. With a resigned lift of her eyebrows my sister hastened away, and I sauntered into the house, through the lounge and out through the french windows to the lawn again. Sinking into a deck chair, I drew out my pipe and began to fill it when Clare came out of the drawing-room and I saw that there was a worried frown between her brows.

"What's up?" I demanded. Clare sighed as she began to stack up the tea things on the trolley preparatory to taking them into the kitchen quarters for washing up.

"Poor old Nannie," she said. "I *am* sorry for her, it's too bad. She'd just finished a big wash—we have to do a good deal of washing here, the children get through so much and the laundry only calls once a fortnight—and hung it up to dry on the line we always use outside the kitchen door, in the vegetable garden. She says she simply can't *think* how it happened, but she supposes she didn't tie the rope securely—but suddenly she happened to glance out of the window and the line of washing had vanished! She rushed out, and there was the whole line of newly washed things flat in the dirt . . . and now the wash has got to be done all over again!"

There was a sound in the room behind us and I glanced

round quickly. Michael stood just within the french windows, listening—and as I glanced I caught a triumphantly
malicious grin on his childish face. It vanished on the instant,
even as I turned my head, but it *had* been there, of that I was
certain, though he faced me innocently, never blinking an
eyelid, and came sauntering out with the most *dégagé* air. As
Clare went round to the kitchen, wheeling her trolley-load of
tea things, I beckoned the child over to me.

He came reluctantly, one cautious eye on me, and I studied
him intently as he stood in the crook of my arm, his small
body rigid, watchful . . . what had happened to the bouncing, happy, noisy little boy I used to know? Against my will,
more and more I was being forced unto realising that there
was a great and fundamental change here. . . .

"Mike," I said, "who were you laughing with up there in
the attic just now?"

Now his glance at me was wary, startled as a wild thing
surprised in its lair! He eyed me sharply, looked away and
did not answer. I repeated my question and at last he spoke
sullenly.

"I wan't there. Don't know what you mean! I been playin'
in the garden . . ."

"I know," I said, "but you *were* there, you know, in the
attic. You went up there after you'd been playing in the
garden. After Nannie's washing had tumbled down. Did you
know about that?"

He hesitated, then nodded as I went on.

"I saw you sitting on the window—laughing and talking to
somebody. Who was it?"

He looked at me with narrowed eyes, obviously undecided,
then answered with a spurt of defiance.

"Why, I was talkin' to Saloozy! That's who I was talkin' to!
And now can I go and play?"

I let him go in silence and watched him dive away into the
bushes. Frankly, I didn't know what to say. Or think . . .

Well, that episode gave me, as the French say, "furiously to
think"—and Sybil's note to me, received the following day,

didn't help to clarify things. She said that she had sounded her husband about the past history of Wichart's Farm, but he knew little more than she did. He simply confirmed Sybil's statement that few people ever stayed long at the farm—no matter how long a lease they had taken, after a while they cut their losses and moved out, giving no definite reason. There had been (he said) since he and Sybil had come to the Hall, three "lets" only. An artist and his wife, then a pair of land-girls who meant to turn the place into a poultry farm, and finally an elderly professor of some sort who had planned to run a coaching establishment for selected pupils. This last tenant had plainly meant to spend the last of his days there, installed himself complete with furniture, cart-loads of books, a cook-housekeeper, two maids, and a secretary-assistant, as well as sixteen pupils, only two years before my sister took the house. But like the others, his tenancy came to an abrupt end and the place had been "to let" again until Clare took it.

Then I decided to go down to the village and try and pump Mrs. Pressing, of Tanfield Post Office. After her cryptic message to Clare I felt positive that she knew a great deal of the "queerness" at Wichart's Farm, if not the story behind it all. But though by this time the old lady and I were on very pleasant terms, as to save my sister I went daily down to the Post Office to post or fetch letters, I drew a blank here likewise.

Mrs. Pressing was politely non-committal—either she knew nothing, or she was determined to give nothing away!

Like Sybil, she admitted that Wichart's didn't seem to be a lucky house in its lettings—tenants wouldn't stay, complained of being disturbed at nights, though this, she was sure, must have been the rats or mice or something like that; old houses often had noises that were difficult to account for. But anything more I could not get out of her, though I was morally certain there was plenty more she *could* have said had she chosen; the guarded, wary nature of her answers gave that away. Either it was, as Sybil had said, the dislike of the native to give away local secrets to a "foreigner"—or possibly a

severe warning had been circulated, by the agents trying
to let the place, to everybody in the neighbourhood who might
repeat stories likely to hinder such letting.

So there we were—no further! And the days wound lazily
on. Nothing else happened, and Michael behaved himself
and worked very hard at his Latin—in which he was making
really amazing progress—and then Nannie's old mother fell
ill, and she had to rush to the rescue. It was only a question of
her being away a few days, as Nannie's sister, who usually
lived with her mother, was on holiday with a friend in
Ireland, and would be returning within a week. However,
until she returned there was nothing for Nannie to do but to
pack her suitcase and go, and though Clare looked gloomy, I
told her to cheer up. It would only be a few days. I promptly
rang up Fortnum and Mason for a load of tinned foods so as
to save Clare as much cooking as possible—Ada could cope
with the rough work, and together we'd manage the children.
Susan could sleep in Clare's room, and I would move Mike's
bed into my room—he could sleep with me until Nannie got
back.

So it was settled—but I wondered why, when during lunch
that day the children were told of the altered sleeping
arrangements, an odd little shadow seemed to cross Michael's
face. He was, I knew, very fond of me—or had been at one
time—and normally speaking, would have regarded a chance
of sharing a room with me as the greatest possible adventure.
But he said nothing and neither did I, and later on I saw him
off with his mother and sister in my car to the Curtis's children's garden party—whither I had been bidden also. But
children's parties are not much in my line, so I excused
myself, and spent the afternoon in the garden with a book.

Some three hours later, from my deck chair outside the
french windows of the lounge I heard the return of the party,
and prepared myself for a tumultuous onslaught from two
excited youngsters, each eager to be the first to tell me all
about the party.

But they did not appear. I concluded that Clare had taken
both her offspring upstairs to wash hands and faces and quite

possibly to change clothes torn or dirtied in the afternoon's romping, and returned to my book—and it was nearly dinner-time when Clare appeared alone, spruce in a fresh frock, but with a harassed frown on her pretty face. As I helped her prepare dinner, she told me—rather abruptly—that Michael had been so naughty at the party that she had forbidden him to come down to dinner as a punishment and sent him to bed, and that Sue being very tired, she had done the same with her. I could see that something was amiss but tactfully said nothing as we ate our meal—mainly consisting of cold Fortnum and Mason products helped out with fresh-cut salad and fruit afterwards—but later on, as we sat smoking and talking in the garden in the warm, sweet-scented dusk of a lovely June night, I put a tentative question. Clare hesitated, then spoke in a profoundly troubled voice.

"You know, Miles, if it wasn't idiotic, I'd be tempted sometimes to think that there was an odd sort of Fate follow-ing anybody who does anything to Mike? I know it *can* only be coincidence, of course . . . but I remember him saying to me once, soon after we came here, when I told him I would have to spank him for some flagrant disobedience, 'You shouldn't, Mummy! Saloozy doesn't like me being hurt.' Of course I told him not to talk nonsense and spanked him all the same. I hate hurting my babies, but Mike's a boy and he's got no father—and I won't have Naunton some day tell-ing me that I've spoilt his son and made him soft because I hadn't the guts to punish him when he was naughty!" She laughed forlornly. "And would you believe it?—only a day or so afterwards I slipped and sprained my ankle and was hob-bling about on a stick for a week at least! And though Mike didn't say, 'I told you so,' he went about with a smug smile a yard wide!"

"*Must* be coincidence—of course," I said.

"I know it must be—really," said Clare. "And if that had been the *only* time I wouldn't have thought again about it. But . . ." she brooded, "that's not the *only* time, Miles! It's really rather odd how often it happens. Once, I remember, Mike fell foul of Ada. She was going out with her young man

on her afternoon off, and she'd brought her best frock and
hat here to change into after she'd done her morning's work.
She'd left the dress and the hat—a fearsome object with a
huge red feather wing arrangement in it sticking up—lying in
the scullery while she did her work. Mike and Sue were
playing Red Indians and—rather naturally but unfortunately!—Mike made off with Ada's feather to make an Indian
war bonnet. Naturally she was furious, and wept and scolded
him and took away from him a toy boat she had given him
only a day or so before as a punishment. And two nights later
on she was drying her hair at the kitchen fire in her mother's
cottage, and somehow her hair caught alight, though it was
still wet—and she lost nearly half of it before her mother
smothered her head with a wet towel and put it out! And
another time little Hugh Lett persuaded Mrs. Pressing at the
Post Office to let him have the last lot of some special sweets
that Mike wanted—those striped bull's-eyes, I think they
were. Mike turned up just as Hughie walked out of the shop
with the bag—and a week later Hughie developed mumps."
She brooded. "Oh, it *must* be coincidence, I know, but it's
queer! It was queer, wasn't it, that Nannie's washing should
have collapsed in the dirt only a little while after she'd lost
her temper with Mike and shaken him? And today . . .
well, Miss Truman, the Curtis's governess, was quite justified
in taking the stick away from Mike. But . . . on the way out
of the Hall some bees suddenly attacked her—only *her,* out
of a whole party!—and the poor girl had to go home with a
face swollen up like a cream puff from the stings!"

I stared at my sister, suddenly alert. "What's all this? What
stick?" I said. "What happened this afternoon?"

"Well," said Clare. "It all started with Sylvia—Sybil's eldest
girl—falling into the pond! Miss Truman wasn't there at the
start of it—she was sitting reading and knitting some way
away from them, letting them play as they wanted, and it
wasn't until Sylvia fell in that she came into things at all. But
it seems, from the children's confused stories, that they were
arguing about fairy tales, and if they were true, and Mike
said magic was true, and *he* knew how to make magic, and

they laughed at him." She wrinkled her pretty brows. "Let's see, who was there? The two Cotter children from the Vicarage and Sybil's three brats, and my two, and the three Lett children and two or three others. Anyway, they were all together, and apparently Sylvia jeered at Mike and he got nettled and pulled out a stick from inside his coat, pointed it at Sylvia and *said* something . . . and the children said that she simply walked straight to the pond and over the edge and in, as though she couldn't help herself! I . . . I don't believe it, of course. I'm sure she simply tumbled in, lost her balance or something . . . but it's odd that the children should all tell the same tale, isn't it? Perry Cotter said she 'went all wooden and didn't look at anything, just walked like a walking doll into the water?'—and Perry is thirteen, and I should imagine, as a parson's child, has been brought up to tell the truth as far as he knows it."

"What happened then?" I demanded.

"Oh," said Clare. "Of course Sylvia woke up and yelled in a panic when she fell into the water, and Miss Truman rushed over and seized the stick from Michael . . . though she says he hung onto it and wrestled furiously to keep it, and was surprisingly strong for a mere baby . . . and she gave it to me. I made Mike say he was very sorry both to her and Sylvia, but I wouldn't give him back the stick, though he begged and begged—and now he's in bed with the sulks!" She laughed self-consciously. "Hope nothing's going to happen to *me* now!"

"Have you got the stick?" I asked. "I'd like to see it."

Clare nodded. "I'll get it. It certainly is unlike anything else I've ever seen." She rose, and going into the lounge, returned in a moment with a slender black rod in her hands. "What do you make of this?"

I examined it curiously. It was certainly an odd thing, and I likewise had never seen anything quite like it before. It was about a foot and a half long—roughly the length of my forearm—and as big round as a slim walking cane. It was more like the old-fashioned round blackwood ruler than anything else . . . but it was plainly *not* a ruler. Round the middle of it were two metal bands, one of copper and one of zinc, inscribed with curious characters, and at one end there was fitted a polyhedral prism cut to triangular shape, and at the other a similar figure in black resin. The rod was gilded at the resin end and silvered at the prism end, and just below each end it was bound with fine black silk. I turned it over and studied the queer characters engraved on the two central bands.

They were not hieroglyphics. They looked more like Nordic runes or early Hebrew characters than anything else, and yet I had an uneasy feeling they were neither runes nor Hebrew . . . I didn't know *what* they were. I studied the thing from end to end, balanced it, weighed it—then suddenly I felt the same sense of *grue* sweep over me that I had felt that unforgettable day in the kitchen garden, and again in the Long Attic; and with a shock like the touch of an electric wire, I knew what it was! I opened my mouth to exclaim but shut it again—for what was the sense of alarming my sister?—pulled myself sharply together and handed the rod back to Clare.

"I haven't any idea what it could be," I lied. "But I should keep it locked up." For a split second I hunted wildly for a good reason to give for saying that—invented wildly and—fortunately—convincingly.

"I believe the last tenant was an old professor of some sort—it probably belonged to him. I should keep it until we can find out where he's gone and can write telling him it's been found. Meantime it's obviously too valuable a thing to let a kid knock about as he likes. And—er—by the way, Clare, where on earth did Mike find it? And how did he manage to carry it to Sybil's without anybody seeing it? It's *much* too long to go into a small boy's pocket, and as he wears shorts he couldn't have carried it down the leg of his trousers, as I used to carry my airgun when I was a boy."

Clare shook her head.

"He persists that it's Saloozy's stick and that Saloozy gave it to him!" she said vexedly. "I *can't* get him out of that idiotic way of talking, try as I may! He says Saloozy 'showed him where to find it' very soon after he came here, but he seems completely—or deliberately—vague as to how, when, or where. And as for carrying it, I found he'd cut a hole in the lining of his jacket just above the breast pocket so that he could slip it in there—the length of the jacket just takes it, with a bit to spare. That's how he managed to take it about with him. And as to how long he's been doing it, I don't know!" She frowned. "Miles, I'm getting worried, honestly I am! In so many little ways Mike's altered—he's so much less open and frank and honest than he was, and it's getting worse instead of better. I don't know what to do. . . . ."

But this was getting on dangerous ground, and I had no intention of letting Mike's mother draw me into a discussion on the general situation! I sent her off to bed with a kiss and a few reassuring generalisations about children going through various odd phases, and that she mustn't worry . . . the usual sort of stuff . . . which comforted her somewhat, and we parted for the night. But as I undressed, stealing a sidelong glance at Mike's small sleeping face on the pillow of his bed by the window, I too felt worried. Where on earth had the child got hold of a real magician's wand—and what was far worse, some definite notion, fantastic as it seemed, of how to use it? "Saloozy's stick"—who and what *was* Saloozy? Dimly behind the growing mystery loomed a dark and sinister Somebody, but just how to track down that somebody, incarnate or discarnate—the latter, I felt sure—I could not think!

With an exasperated sigh I turned out the light, slipped into bed, and composed myself to sleep . . . but sleep would not come. I tossed and turned from side to side, pondering, worrying, analysing, alternately telling myself that Clare and I were fools and that all we were doing was to allow a set of odd coincidences to build themselves into a bogeyman that had no existence in fact, and telling myself bluntly that the damn house had a jinx on it, and that whatever the reason, Clare had better cut her losses and get out of it, like the other tenants. But—how was I to explain myself to her, if I gave her this advice? I'd nothing definite to go on—and the poor little soul had sunk every penny she possessed in the place and, was so happy and contented there, settled for the first time in years, and looking forward to a future in which I was already beginning to suspect Alan Hemingway would play a part. If I could only "lay" the jinx, release the house—and Mike—from the presence that was looming over both! I was still awake, worrying and fretting over the problem, when I was conscious of a faint movement from the direction of Mike's bed.

I all but called out "Mike, are you awake?" but something held me back and I remained silent, watching and listening. The room was not wholly in darkness, as the curtains were not fully drawn and there was a bright moon.

A shaft of moonlight lay across the foot of Michael's little bed and extended along the floor to the door, and as I watched I saw the small figure of the child cross the strip of moonlight as he went towards the door. Beside the door he paused, one small hand on the handle, and looked back in the direction of my bed as though to assure himself that I was sleeping—he was standing then full in the moonlight and I saw that he was fully awake, though the first idea that had flashed across my mind was that he might be walking in his sleep. But the look he was directing towards where I lay in the shadows was the look of someone fully and vitally conscious, a look both cunning and triumphant, and I suddenly realised that he had been awake all the time, probably ever since I came up to bed, merely biding his time until I went to sleep and he could creep out of the room! He must have exercised the most unchild-like patience and self-control to have feigned sleep so successfully for so long, and I felt an odd little shiver touch me.

He waited a full minute, then softly opened the door and, leaving it open, went off down the moonlit passage outside—and I was out of my bed in a flash and peering after him! The small blue pyjama-clad figure was just turning the corner of the attic stairs that led to the mysterious top floor, and pausing only a moment to thrust my feet into soft slippers, as I knew the rough, splintery surface of those uncarpeted stairs, I stole after him. What on earth could be

taking the boy up to that great empty room at this time of
night . . . what was he going to do? With the feeling strong
upon me that if I were wise and cautious I might at last be
given a chance to solve this dark mystery, I waited a few
minutes to let the child get well ahead of me, and softly
followed him.

As the attic stairs ran directly up in one long steep flight, if
he had turned his head he must have seen me, so I hung back
for a few minutes to let him get to the top of the stairs, and
then followed swiftly. As I reached the top of the stairs, there
was no sign of Michael—he had gone on into the Long Attic,
luckily leaving the door ajar—and I noted thankfully that the
closet door was open likewise, which would be useful in case I
needed a quick retreat and had no time to get downstairs. I
tip-toed down the passage and peered through the crack of
the attic door into the long room.

I could hear the murmur of Michael's voice, and presently
I saw that he was sitting on the sill of the dormer window
nearest the fireplace—the one where he had been sitting when
Sybil and I had seen him from the garden—clear in the bright
moonlight, that paved the floor of the old attic with oblong
sections of alternate silver and black. And he was talking—
talking, volubly, anxiously, to—nothing at all!

That is, *I* could see nothing—nothing and nobody—but
that *Mike* could see somebody was plain. It was also plain
that he was hearing somebody speak, though I heard nothing.
In between his eager talk he paused, plainly to listen to some
response, nodded, frowned, protested, exclaimed, then took
up his tale again, precisely as though he was talking to a
palpable living person . . . yet the pauses in his speech were
simply pauses to me. It was as though the boy were talking to
himself, "making pretend" to be answered, as we used to say
in our childhood. Yet—*was* it pretence? I listened with pain-
ful intensity. The child was talking about the Curtis tea
party.

"They *laughed,* Saloozy . . . and it made me mad! I told
them I knew how to make magic . . . that you'd taught me
and you were going to teach me more, *much* more, and they

laughed at me . . . serves me right for talking! Oh dear, I
know you don't like it, but it's so difficult to help it when
silly people laugh and won't believe you're real! I got mad
and pointed the stick at Sylvia and said the words you taught
me, and it worked! She got stiff all over, and her eyes went
blank and queer, and she just walked right into the water,
and I called out 'now you see I was right' to them all! Only
they were scared and crying out, and Sylvia woke up when
she got into the water and started screaming and that Miss
Truman came running and she was so angry when they told
her that she smacked me—*hard*!"

There was a pause. The child's head was bent as though
listening intently—I could hear nothing, but after a moment
he nodded his head as though assenting and chuckled in a
manner curiously unpleasant to hear.

"Oh yes, she took it away . . . called it a ruler and said I
was playing at being a magician and trying to frighten the
children with it. She gave it to Mummy—but before she took
it away I held onto it hard and *wished* inside myself that
something nasty could happen to her soon, and it *did!*" The
sinister little chuckle came again. "You never let me down,
do you, Saloozy? You ought to have seen her hopping and
squealing when those bees stung her . . . they had to put
her to bed and send for the doctor. Ha, ha, ha!"

The chuckle expanded into a shrill titter of unholy mirth,
and now I felt that I could—almost!—see the Something, the
Someone whom the child, with his keener psychic sight, saw
whole and complete. I knew without the shadow of a doubt
now that Someone old, old and hideously evil, wise not only
in all the wickedness of this world but in the dark and unholy
knowledge of another world as well, had for his own ends
fastened on this innocent child, and my whole heart rose in
disgust and revolt, resolved somehow to save him! I controlled myself with a huge effort, though my head was whirl-
ing with disgust and horror, and I remained rigid behind the
door, watching and listening as Michael went on.

"Yes, and that's what I'm worried about, Saloozy.

Mummy's got your stick, your magic stick that you lent me, and she's locked it up and I can't get at it to use again! And I was getting on so well with it! And I'm practising looking in that bit of mirror I found, though the pictures aren't coming *very* clearly just yet—it'll be better when you let me use the Ball. And I'm learning that Latin you wanted me to learn so that I'll soon be able to read the Black Book and learn all the spells that control Them when They come, and then I shall want your magic stick more and more." He paused a moment and then drew a sigh of relief. "Oh, I'm so glad . . . you'll get it back for me? I'll hide it in the ash tree again—I can't carry it about with me any more 'cos Mummy found the place where I hide it in my coat; or if you think the ash tree isn't safe any more, will you tell me a place to hide it—a real secret place? And when I'm ready to use them you'll show me where to find the Book and the Ball? Oh, that will be lovely . . . thank you, thank you! Now I'll go back to bed and to sleep, shall I? Good night, Saloozy . . . good night!"

Slipping off the window sill the child made a curious sort of salute, waited a moment as though to see whether this invisible companion had truly gone, and came running down the long room towards the door—I stepped hastily into the little closet and drew the door to, and heard him go past and down the stairs. After waiting a few minutes I went down myself and going softly into the bathroom next to my room, emerged making a great clatter with the door handle so that had he, on entering the room, noticed my absence I would be ready with an excuse. But when I went in he was—apparently, at all events—sound asleep. But *I* had precious little sleep that night. . . .

I didn't feel any better next morning when I asked Clare to let me have another look at the curious stick or ruler that young Michael had been carrying about, and she found—though she swore she hadn't touched the drawer of her writing-table in which I had seen her lock the stick—that it was no longer there! Neither was it—for I went to look—in the hollow at the base of the ash tree where at one time Mike had been in the habit of keeping it—where (I gathered after) he had first found it. It had simply disappeared.

Clare was puzzled, I could see, when I asked her to take Mike out to tea somewhere that afternoon. But she asked no questions, and said she would take my car and drive over to the Vicarage to call and take Mike with her. He pulled rather a long face—it took a great deal of persuasion or a direct command to get him to leave the Farm these days—but they duly set off, and the moment they were out of sight I went upstairs hot-foot to the attic. Having had some experience by now of Mike's uncanny prescience, with him in the house I could never be sure of having a good long time to myself up there undisturbed. But today I meant to explore that room— the core and centre, I was sure, of the house's "queerness"— and I shut the door behind me and advanced down the long dusty, sun-dappled room with a curious feeling of trepidation, as though I were going to meet a mortal enemy . . . and truth to tell, by this time I was by no means sure I was *not*!

One thing I *was* sure of—that the main focus of the Force that Mike called "Saloozy" lay somewhere at the far end of the room, by the old fireplace. It was there I had felt that first instinctive sense of "withdrawal" and there I had always lingered longest—and it was at the far end, the fireplace end, of the room that I had twice seen Michael talking to some-body. Standing before the gaping, blackened hollow that had been the old fireplace, staring at it and the fragments of rusted iron that projected from the wall beside it, my eyes travelled up to the brick mantelpiece that ran along the projecting chimney-breast above the fireplace, and the square carved wooden frame containing the silly "Christmas An-nual" picture that was fixed to the brickwork above it.

I found myself staring again at this picture and wondering afresh why such a cheap and stupid print should have been considered worthy of a handsome carved wooden frame, a frame that had—unless my eyes deceived me—even once been gilded? I leant forward to examine it closer and saw with a start of surprise that the print was not, as on a cursory glance I had thought, actually *enclosed* in the frame. The original picture was still in the frame—the print had merely been pasted over it. Pasted on neatly enough, with its edges cut flush with the frame, but age had made the paper begin to dry and break away, here and there bits had cracked and curled up, showing the foundation to which it had been stuck. Curious and interested, I took out my pocket knife and did a little prising, and found the paper so brittle with age that without difficulty I tore several large pieces away, and found that underneath the paper was an oil painting of some sort. A portrait, it seemed. I could see part of a hand resting on a desk or table, the fragment of a velvet dress or cloak of some sort.

Much thrilled, I dashed down to the kitchen for some warm water and a soft cloth, and in a few minutes the last shreds of paper were rubbed away and the hidden picture exposed to view.

It was a carefully painted portrait—not a work of genius, but vivid enough and, one felt, probably a good likeness of the original, an elderly man in Elizabethan dress, starched ruff and dark green velvet doublet, with a pointed grey beard and moustache, long grizzled hair, and small piercing dark eyes that stared straight out of the canvas. It was an old painting, dark and cracked here and there with age, but otherwise undamaged—the subject stood three-quarter length, resting one hand on a table, on which could dimly be seen what looked like a glass ball on a stand, an open book, and a skull. Over one shoulder a black cloak hung, half concealing the other hand, which was placed on his hip—but in that hand could be seen a slender dark stick, with a curious triangular tip and about the middle double-ringed with metal. The Wand! The Wand I had handled, the Wand that had so mysteriously vanished from my sister's writing desk! With a confused sense that somehow I had uncovered, or was in process of uncovering, something that while strange and dreadful, did not surprise me, I stared, transfixed, at the painted face, narrow, evil, wrinkled, with those rapier-like

black eyes that bored into mine . . . and there came a flurry
of steps into the room behind me and Michael, breathless,
furious, flung himself fiercely upon me, fighting, biting,
pummelling like a wild creature!

"I knew it, I felt it . . . Saloozy brought me back to stop
you! That's him—that's Saloozy! Look how he's frowning,
how angry he is! You shall not, you mustn't—get away Uncle
Miles! This is Saloozy's place . . . Saloozy . . ."

The child was utterly hysterical, almost foaming at the
mouth—despite his frantic fighting I picked him up, clipping
his arms firmly to his sides, and carried him downstairs,
where Clare, shaking her head with bewilderment, adminis-
tered a bromide tablet and hot milk and put him to bed. It
was only when I promised that I would not go up to the Long
Attic again without him that at last he consented to settle
down, and exhausted with excitement, fell asleep—and it was
only then that I found time to ask my sister what had happened to bring them back so early. I was frankly furious! I
knew that I had had my fingers on the very brink of prying
open this mysterious Saloozy business when Michael had
rushed in, and Clare's explanation did nothing to clear things
up—except that it confirmed my suspicion that something
more than mere coincidence had brought Mike back in time
to stop my explorings in that upper room!

It appeared that halfway to the Vicarage the car had
stopped dead and refused to move! Clare, who was as capable
a driver as she was many other things, had climbed out and
tinkered with the engine, tested the petrol supply, done everything she could, but failed to find anything wrong; and as
just then somebody came along and offered to give them a
tow, Clare decided it would be better to return home—when
lo, just before they reached the Farm the car suddenly re-
asserted itself and they had come home under their own
steam! Whatever had gone wrong had suddenly decided to go
right . . . *directly they were almost home again!* And the
moment they turned into the gates, Michael had flung himself pellmell out of the car and, without a word to his mother,
had run into the house and upstairs like a wild thing. . . .

I made light of the scene in the attic, for Clare's sake, pretending that the child had merely been in a panic for fear I had interfered with some of his possessions left up there; and as it was now getting on for seven o'clock I left her to put Baby to bed and cope with the preparing of the dinner, thanking the gods as she did so that Nannie was returning on the morrow. I was quite determined to complete my search of the attic room that had been so rudely interrupted! But in order to do it in peace I would have to see that I was not disturbed again. . . .

Michael was still sleeping when I went softly into my room, and my heart contracted with pity as I looked at him— he was palpably thinner and paler than when I first came, and there were dark rings under his eyes and traces of tears on his cheeks. As I rummaged in my suitcase I sent up a mental prayer to the Higher Powers that I might be helped to rescue this child from the dark and alien Entity from the Outer World that he called "Saloozy"—that Entity who had, I was certain, once walked the earth in the person of the subject of that old portrait. I soon found what I was looking for—a little silver chain from which hung a silver Crucifix. It had been given to me by a woman I dearly loved—the woman for whose sake I had remained a bachelor. She took the veil and disappeared from the world of men, and I never moved without the last present she gave me. I slipped the chain through the buttonhole of his pyjamas—not daring, for fear of waking him, to raise his head to put it round his neck—and tied it fast. As I did so I had to pull back the bedclothes a little, as he had burrowed like a little mole beneath them— and I gasped with astonishment. For there, gleaming sullenly up at me like a slim black snake, close to the child's body, lay the Wand! "Saloozy's stick"!

Saloozy had been as good as his word, and given it back to his pupil. Even somehow drawing it out of a locked drawer to do so . . . what do the experts on psychic phenomena call it?

"Dematerialisation." The passage of matter through matter. . . .

As I drew the evil thing out it felt cold to my touch, cold and deadly, though it had been lying close to the warm body of the sleeping child.

I held it firmly in my left hand, for I was taking no chances of its being spirited away again if I laid it down for a moment! I bent over Michael and drew the fingers of my right hand softly over his forehead, over and back, over and back . . . I was no novice, thank God, at hypnotism, and though I knew I was pitting my still-young knowledge of magic against Something cunning and powerful in the extreme, whose knowledge of that same magic had been perfected through centuries of experience, yet I could not help feeling that with the forces of good on my side, I would be helped to succeed.

As I stroked the child's forehead I *willed* as hard as I knew how for him to lie still until I had done what I meant to do. I willed him to lie and sleep, under the protection of the Cross, to sleep peacefully until I bade him awaken, and as I stroked I felt that cold and horrible *grue* steal round me, as Something hovered near, furious, baffled . . . sensing, or so I hoped, defeat and banishment ahead. . . .

As I straightened up, satisfied that I had put Michael to sleep until I chose that he should waken, I turned a ring I always wear—one I got in the East, in Persia, that is inscribed with the Seal of Solomon, which is potent against Evil—three times, and holding firmly to the Wand I mounted the stairs again towards the attic.

The air was charged with menace as I went in—menace clear and unmistakable. The very tensity of the dead silence proclaimed it—Something awaited me! Something was going to fight—and I was going to accept the challenge! I would not let myself think what might happen if I lost . . . but I did not intend to lose. Within the last ten minutes a new and amazing confidence had come to me, and with a firm step I entered the sinister attic, walked up to the picture and tried to drag it from the wall. That damned portrait for so long safely hidden behind the silly print pasted over it, but exercising its dire influence in secret from behind—that portrait was the heart of the curse that plainly hung over Wichart's Farm, and I was determined to get rid of the thing, if I had to chop it out of the wall piecemeal!

The frame was firmly clamped to the wall and I could not find a single place where one might insert a knife to try and prise it off, though I tried several places with the big blade of my pocket knife . . . wondering if I should go downstairs and get a chisel, I went feeling inch by inch round the edge of the carved frame, pressing and pulling, and somehow I must have touched a secret spring, for with a harsh click the picture swung out towards me! It swung out as the door of a small safe swings when it is opened, and I saw that the picture had been fixed to the door—which it most effectively hid—of a little shallow cupboard sunk in the thick brickwork of the chimney-breast. A cupboard in where were three small dark bundles. . . .

As it swung open there was a sharp grinding sound overhead and out of sheer instinct I sprang back, only just in time to miss a great lump of plaster that had detached itself from the ceiling and fell plump on the place where I had been standing. Had I not moved just in time the thing must have caught me full on the head and either badly damaged or quite possibly killed me! I was rather shaken as I stared at the fallen plaster. Plainly the Being I was fighting was desperate, but oddly enough, that realisation heartened me enormously. If he were desperate, then it meant I was "getting warm" as the children say! Nay, I was getting more than warm, I was on the very edge of unravelling the mystery . . . unless the mysterious bundles inside the little cupboard lied!

The room was silent, the Force exhausted for the moment by its tremendous effort of malice as I swept the bundles into my arms and carried them over to the fading light by the dormer window.

Wrapped in a tattered piece of old green damask was a large book, its ancient black leather cover wrapped and damaged. It bore upon its back a curious Sign, and as I opened the yellowed pages I saw they were inscribed in heavy black-letter Latin, ornamented here and there with red capitals and

interleaved with carefully drawn diagrams. I read a few lines
and shut the book, shuddering. The Grimoire! The Black
Book—I had suspected it. The Book of Spells, of evil magic,
in the working of which a little child was to be trained! In
the tense silence of the room I hastily unwrapped the two
other bundles. In one was a human skull, coloured to the
tinge of old ivory by the centuries that had passed over it;
and last of all, in a battered leather bag that was falling to
pieces with age, was a rusted metal stand, and beside it a
round and shining glass ball—a crystal. I laid "Saloozy's stick"
beside the three and looked soberly at them—I knew now
what I had to face! The spirit, dead but still evilly, wickedly
alive, of the old magician whose picture I had unveiled. The
Ball, the Book, the Skull, and the Wand . . . going up to
the fireplace again I seized the loosely swinging door of the
cupboard to which the picture was fixed in my hands and
wrenched savagely. The hellish portrait should burn, and all
the other things with it—only so would the Farm be cleansed
and whole!

I wrenched and wrenched again, with all my strength—and
I am a sixfooter, broad in proportion, and I flung all my
weight into it—but it took every ounce of strength I could
bring to bear on that frail square of wood before at last, with
a creak and a groan that was like a cry of mortal agony, it
parted from its hinges! Heaping the other oddments upon it,
I ran like a hare out of the room and down the stairs, and
only just in time, as with a roar of falling plaster and woodwork another part of the roof above the door gave way and
came cascading down into the room just as I leapt out into
the passage! It was only thanks to the fact that I wore the
Ring of Solomon that I didn't get killed. . . .

I was panting like a winded horse when I got downstairs—
I'd had enough, and more than enough, but my task was not
over yet. I didn't realise as I went through the kitchen, where
Clare was fussing over the stove, how odd I was looking—she
told me afterwards. White-faced, and streaked with dust and
dirt, and streaming with perspiration . . . she said some-

thing to me as I went through but I wasn't stopping for anybody now!

I knew there was plenty of rubbish—sticks, old papers, dry grass and weeds, straw bottle-covers, dead branches, cardboard boxes—all sorts of things that would burn quickly—round by the tool shed. I piled the stuff together as fast as I could though I could only use one hand—I held tight to those unholy things with the other, I literally didn't dare put 'em down for fear they might be swept away when my back was turned! I lit a match, and after several failures the heap blazed up and when it was really roaring high, I raked a hollow in it and stuffed the devilish things in amongst the flames regardless of singed eyebrows and burnt hands. And I didn't quit until everything except the crystal ball was burnt to ashes and I'd stamped and scattered every one of those—and the ball I dropped down the well and rejoiced to hear the splash that meant its end.

The fire burned oddly high and furiously, and more than once I was glad I'd lighted it on a wide empty patch of ground, as flaming brands kept leaping out and landing far and wide, as though in a futile endeavour to reach and set light to something—the house for preference! But though two or three landed on the roof of the tool shed, I managed to pull them off with the garden rake and beat them out before they got going, and more than one came leaping out in my direction with a fierceness that was more than chance. But luck—or maybe something greater—was my way, and those evil things, and the picture of their one-time owner, vanished forever . . . and as I had foreseen, the Farm was clean again.

Michael slept peacefully through it all. I awakened him when I went up to change and wash—I was as black as a sweep and as exhausted as though I'd run a mile!—and it was plain from the moment he woke up that the old Michael was back again. The old jolly, romping, ordinary little boy. Gone was his interest in Latin, his love of solitude, his talk of "Saloozy" . . . and Clare told me only two days later that she couldn't imagine why she hadn't liked the Long Attic! It would make a first-class playroom for the children in winter or for wet days. When the damage had been repaired she was going to have it properly painted and done up and a stove installed and proper electric light, and put some plain furniture and all the children's toys and books in it. It would be a god-send to have a place like that to park them in when one really wanted peace. . . .

But before I went back to London I walked down to Tanfield Post Office on the pretext of getting some tobacco, and found Mrs. Pressing working in her little garden. Leaning over the fence I looked her straight in the eyes and said:

"Look here, Mrs. Pressing, I know you wouldn't talk to me when I tried to make you once before, but I think you can now. The ghost—or whatever you like to call it—at the Farm, is laid! I've laid it."

She straightened up from the clump of purple phlox over which she was bending and looked sharply at me as I went on.

"I'm going back to London. It's all over, and I'm never going to say anything about it to *anybody*. Least of all to my sister, who's as happy as a queen there, and the children too. But . . . if you'd like to be nice enough to ask me in for a pipe and a glass of that good damson wine you once gave me to taste, perhaps you might like to hear what happened. And in return, perhaps you could tell me some of what you *didn't* tell me when I last tried to talk to you about all this!"

In the quiet little kitchen of the cottage, with a fat hand planted on each knee and her shrewd eyes fixed on my face, the old lady listened intently as I told my tale, and when I came to the end she drew a long sigh of thankfulness.

"So, he's beat at last—the Lord be praised! And you too, sir." She looked at me almost reverently. "You was brave, sir—there was danger, I know. It's always had a bad name, Wichart's—we children used to go there sometimes in the daytime for 'dares,' but not one of us 'ud go there a' nights, and it was never let for long at a time. We used to say the ghost chased 'em out—anyway, they went. When I got married

I went away to live in London, and my husband laughed me out of believing in such things. So when I was widowed and came back here, I went as cook at Wichart's, to a right nice young couple who'd taken it—but it wasn't long before I knew I was right and he was wrong! I was sorry for them two, and I stayed as long as they did—more for her than for him; she was a nice young lady. An artist and his wife they were, Mr. and Mrs. Abbott. Quite young, with three pretty children, and as happy as kings. But that old wicked one in the picture, he got into the husband and nothing ever went right after. Mr. Abbott took to learning Latin and trying to look into the crystal and studying bad old books, just like you say that blessed child did. And I used to hear Mrs. Abbott sobbin' in the night while he was up there in the Long Attic—that's where the badness stems from in that house."

"I know," I said. "But *who* started it all? You spoke of 'he.'"

"I'll tell you in a minute, but don't hurry me!" She looked at me reprovingly. "I didn't rightly know the story, time the Abbotts was there; but I pieced it together as time went on, talking to the older folks and them as remembered the tales about Wichart's their granmas and granpas used to tell. . . . So after a while I reckon I knew pretty well what set all the mischief going—but I don't talk about it—t'ain't a pretty story. Poor Mr. Abbott! Poor young gentleman, learnin' the devil only knows what, with *That* standing over him teachin' and urging him, so that the awful things *He* knew about could go on bein' done. So that He could go on workin' through somebody. . . ."

She drew a long sigh.

"They parted company at last, Mr. and Mrs Abbott—poor young folks. She couldn't stand it no more, she was that scared, and she up and went away and took the children; and Mr. Abbott, he went away and joined some sort of dreadful Brotherhood, I heard tell, that goes in for this kind of stuff. If there *is* such Brotherhoods, that is, which I'd hate to believe. . . ."

"I'm afraid there *are* Black Brotherhoods as well as White," I said. "What about the other tenants? Were they all 'influenced' in the same way?"

"Well," said the old lady. *"Somebody* out of every lot o' people that ever went to live there seemed to turn queer and bad, no matter how nice they might be to start with—I suppose *He* found some easier to get hold of than others. When Mr. and Mrs. Abbott left, there was two young ladies come. One didn't feel anything at all, but the other used to talk to me by the hour about how she hated the place and how scared she was, though she didn't know what of; and finally they took to quarrelling and fighting, them that was the greatest friends, and if it hadn't been that one of them's mother fell ill and they had to leave I don't know how it 'ud have ended. I heard tell afterwards that when they got away they was fast friends again, so they left in time. And then a professor took it—a 'coach' they called him—with a bunch of pupils. And with the professor and his young gentlemen, the taint touched several of *them*—maybe becuase they was young and easy to influence. They say they got up to trying witch-stuff together in the Long Attic, and scared one so that he jumped out o' the window and broke his hip and got lamed for life, and another tried to hang himself. So the professor got scared and they all left, and I don't wonder!"

"Nor do I," I said. "But, tell me, Mrs. Pressing, why 'Saloozy.' That's what the child always called him."

"His name was Sir Lucian Fairfax," said the old lady. "But the villagers, they called him 'Sir Lucifer' because they said he sold his soul to the Devil for power to do wickedness. And I make no doubts that's what young Master Michael's mean-ing to say with his 'Saloozy.' "

"I see," I said, "Sir Lucifer—'Saloozy'—ah yes, that's plain enough. Now go on and tell me about Sir Lucifer. Has he ever been *seen,* do you know?"

Mrs. Pressing shook her head.

"Not that I've ever heard about," she said. "There's noises and shadows and *feelings,* if you take my meaning—but it's mostly the effect on people that lives there that gives the place such a bad sort of name. I suppose it's his wicked spirit working on people somehow to make 'em serve the Devil that he served all his life."

"And he lived when?" I hinted.

"Well," said the old lady, "I misremember my dates, but it was in the reign of the Queen who had the other Queen's head cut off—and a dreadful thing that was to do to a Queen, to my mind."

I nodded. Elizabeth I . . . well, well, Saloozy dated from a long time back, that was certain! Mrs. Pressing went on.

"Well, they say this Sir Lucian was a big figure at the Court then; but tales went round about his playing with Black Magic and consorting with those who had to do with it and he was banished here down to the country. He had a fair young wife, too, it's said, but because of his wicked ways she fled from him and went back to her kinsfolk—and none said her nay or sent her back to her husband—so it looks as though she'd good reason to leave him, don't it, sir?"

"It does indeed," I said. "Go on, Mrs. Pressing. This is *most* interesting."

"Well," said the old lady, "he sent a message after her saying that she could go to hell for all he cared, but that he'd see to it that no man ever found her beautiful any more! And sure enough, within a year the poor lass fell ill of a mysterious disease that left her pretty face all twisted up one side so that she looked like one of they masks the children use to frighten each other on Guy Fawkes' Night. And so his words came true! And of course the whisper went round he'd done it with his evil spells. Maybe so and maybe not—but there it is, it happened just as he'd said.

"Then he filled her place with one painted poppet after another, and the Hall with boon companions from God knows where—and in the Dower House, where my lady his mother had lived until a year or two earlier, he built himself what they call a—lobar—laboratory where he could go in secret and carry on his ugly experiments, and nobody would know. I think he did that because there was a lot of talk about him now, and he maybe thought it 'ud be safer to move his wizard things out of the Hall in case there was an accusation made, and a search—anyway, that's what he did. He put an old deaf and dumb woman in to look after the Dower House, and her young grandson he paid to help him in his work—to light the fires and blow the bellows and run errands and all that—and after his drunken friends had fallen into their beds he'd creep down from the Hall and lock himself into his sorcerer's room at the top of the Dower House and work away at his wicked tricks . . . but the Lord got on his track at last, and serve him right!

"This poor lad—Martin was his name—was mortally afraid of him; but he was a sharp lad and couldn't fail to see that what he was doing was against God and man. So at last he couldn't bear it no more, and decided to run away and take the magician's Wand with him, thinking that without it he couldn't do no more harm. He stole it all right, and he hid it—but Sir Lucian was on his track, and caught him and thrashed him to within an inch of his life and left him lying bleeding and half-dead in a ditch because he wouldn't say where the Wand was hid—and there his old grandmother found him. And deaf and dumb as she was, she made shift to let the villagers know what had happened, and they rose in a body, they did, and marched up to the Hall and set fire to it that very night! They'd suspicioned the lord for a long time— and with poor little Martin bleeding and dying on their hands, they'd got the excuse they were looking for. I've heard it was a sight to see, the painted women and their drunken men coming running screaming out of the doors and windows like rabbits being bolted from a wheat field at harvest time— but it wasn't them the villagers was after! They let 'em run— and waited for the lord; and when he come out, blazing mad with rage, they chased him back into the fire, and so he died, cursing to the last. Seemingly they didn't know about that— lab—laboratory though, or the Dower House 'ud 'a gone up in flames too. Martin couldn't tell 'em, for he died a couple days after the Hall was burnt, and his grandmother went queer in the head and was taken off to a lunatic place—so there wasn't anybody to tell about it.

"But all the same, there must have been a sort of whisper about it because it was always called the Wizard's House; and that got twisted into 'Wichart's'—do you see, sir?"

"Indeed I see," I said. "Yes, that falls into place all right—it does indeed!" I stared before me, for I was thinking deeply, and I was startled when my old hostess put my thoughts into words.

"You know, sir, when I heard about this queerness of Master Michael's—which he never had when he first come here, that I swear!—I began to think of that other boy, little Martin, who'd worked for the wizard Sir Lucian, and died through him. It seemed queer, Master Michael finding the Wand that has been hid all those years—and I wondered if that old devil had been biding his chance and fastened on the child's mind, to sort of infect him with his old wicked knowledge, and maybe train him to his own old ways?" She looked at me reflectively. "I don't know what *you* think, sir, but I've heard that some clever people think as we come back to live on earth many times. Maybe Master Michael was that village lad that worked with Sir Lucian once, and maybe that made him sort of easier to get hold of . . . what do you think?"

I thought a good many things, but I had no time to spend discussing them with the worthy soul. I thanked her for her excellent wine and for her interesting story, which had cleared up many points for me, and drove away, very thoughtful. Some people often have a surprising gift for getting at the heart of things; and her suggestion—it was scarcely sufficiently developed to be called a theory—would certainly explain Michael's curiously clear memory of an ancient laboratory. Thank goodness, though, it was all over, a thing of the past. But truly, "there are more things . . ."

HERODES REDIVIVUS

A. B. L. Munby

I DON'T suppose that many people have heard of Charles
Auckland, the pathologist, as he isn't the type of man who
catches the public eye. What slight reputation he has got is of
rather a sinister nature; for he has always tended to avoid the
broad, beaten tracks of scientific research, and has branched
off to bring light into certain dark cul-de-sacs of the human
mind, which many people feel should be left unilluminated.
Not that one would suspect it from his appearance. Some
men who spend their lives studying abnormalities begin to
look distinctly queer themselves, but not Auckland. To look
at him one would put him down as a country doctor, a big
red-faced man of about sixty, obviously still pretty fit, with a
shrewd but kindly face. We belonged to the same club and
for years had been on nodding terms, but I didn't discover
until quite recently that he was a book-collector, and that
only accidentally. I went to refer to Davenport's *Armorial
Bookbindings* in the club library, and found him reading it.
He deplored its inaccuracies, and I offered to lend him a list
of corrections and additions that I had been preparing. This
led to further discussion on bindings, and finally he invited
me to go back with him to his flat and see his books. It was
not yet ten o'clock and I agreed readily.

The night was fine, and we strolled together across the
park to Artillery Mansions, where he was living at the time.
On arriving we went up in the lift, and were soon seated in

the dining-room of his flat, the walls of which were lined with books from floor to ceiling. I was glad to see that one alcove was entirely filled with calf and vellum bindings, the sight of which sent a little thrill of expectation down my spine. I crossed the room to examine them, and my host rose too. A glance showed me that they were all of the class that second-hand booksellers classify comprehensively under the word "Occult." This, however, did not surprise me, as I knew of Auckland's interests. He took down several volumes, and began to expatiate on them—some first editions of the astro-logical works of Robert Fludd, and a very fine copy of the 1575 *Theatrum Diabolorum*. I expressed my admiration, and we began to talk of trials for witchcraft. He had turned aside to fetch a copy of Scot's *Discoverie* to illustrate some point in his argument when suddenly my eye became riveted on the back of a small book on the top shelf, and my heart missed a beat. Of course it couldn't be, but it was fantastically like it! The same limp vellum cover without any lettering, with the same curious diagonal tear in the vellum at the top of the spine. My hand shook a little as I took it down and opened it. Yes, it was the book. I read once more the title villainously printed on indifferent paper: *Herodes Redivivus seu Liber Scelerosae Vitae et Mortis Sanguinolentae Retzii, Monstri Nannetensis*, Parisiis, MDXLV. As I read the words mem-ories came flooding back of that macabre episode which had overshadowed my schooldays. Some of the terror that had come to me twenty years before returned, and I felt quite faint.

"I say, you must have a nose for a rarity," said Auckland, pointing to the volume in my hand.

"I've seen this book before," I replied.

"Really?" he said. "I'd be very glad to know where. There's no copy in any public collection in England, and the only one I've traced on the Continent is in the Ambrosian Library at Milan. I haven't even *seen* that. It's in the cata-logue, but it's one of those books that librarians are very reluctant to produce. Can you remember where you've met it before?"

"I mean that I've seen this copy before," I answered.

He shook his head dubiously. "I think you must be mistaken about that. I've owned this for nearly twenty years, and before that it was the property of a man that you're most unlikely to have met. In fact, he died in Broadmoor fifteen years ago. His name was—"

"Race," I interposed.

He looked at me with interest. "I shouldn't have expected you to remember that," he said. "You must have been at school during the trial—not that it got much publicity. Thank God, there's legislation to prevent the gutter press from splashing that sort of stuff across their headlines." He half smiled. "You must have been a very precocious child— surely you were only a schoolboy at the time?"

"Yes," I replied. "I was a schoolboy—*the* schoolboy, one might say; the one who gave evidence at the trial and whose name was suppressed."

He put down the book he was holding and looked hard at me. "That's most extraordinarily interesting. I suppose you wouldn't be willing to tell me about it? As you know, cases of that sort are rather my subject. Of course, it would be in the strictest confidence."

I smiled. "There's nothing in my story that I'm particularly ashamed of," I replied, "though I must confess that I occasionally feel that if I'd been a little more intelligent the tragedy might have been averted. However, I've no objection at all. It's only of academic interest now. I haven't thought about the matter for years."

He sat me down in an armchair and poured me out a large whisky-and-soda, then settled himself opposite me.

"Take your time about it," he said. "I'm a very late bird, and it's only a quarter to eleven."

I took a long drink and collected my thoughts.

"I was at a large school on the outskirts of Bristol," I began, "and was not quite sixteen at the time of these events. Even in those days I was extremely interested in old books, a hobby in which I was encouraged by my housemaster. I never cut a great figure on the games field, and when it was wet or I was not put down for a game, I used to go book-hunting in Bristol. Of course, my purse was very limited and my ignorance profound, but I got enormous pleasure out of pottering round the shops and stalls of the town, returning every now and then with a copy of Pope's *Homer* or Theobald's *Shakespeare* to grace my study.

"I don't know whether you're acquainted with Bristol, but it's a most fascinating town. As one descends the hills towards the Avon, one passes from the Georgian crescents and squares of Clifton into the older maritime town, with its magnificent churches and extensive docks. Down by the river are many narrow courts and alleys, which are unchanged since the days when Bristol was a thriving mediaeval port. Much of this poorer area was out of bounds to the boys at school, but having exhausted the bookshops of the University area, I found it convenient to ignore this rule and explored every corner of the old town. One Saturday afternoon—it was in a summer term—I was wandering round the area between St. Mary Redcliffe and the old 'Floating Harbour,' and I discovered a little court approached through a narrow passage. It was a miserable enough place, dark and damp, but a joy to the antiquarian—so long as he didn't have to live there! The first floors of the half-timbered houses jutted out and very nearly shut out the sky, and the court ended abruptly in a high blank wall. At the end on the right was a shop—at least the ground-floor window was filled with a collection of books. They were of little interest, and from the accumulation of dust upon them it was obvious that they hadn't been disturbed for years. The place had a deserted air, and it was in no great hope of finding it open that I tried the door. But it did open, and I found myself in its dark interior. Books were everywhere—all the shelves were blocked by great stacks of books on the floor with narrow lanes through which one could barely squeeze sideways, and over everything lay the same thick coating of dust that I'd noticed in the window. I felt as though I were the first person to enter it for years. No bell rang as I opened the door, and I looked round for the proprietor. I saw him sitting in an alcove at my right, and I picked my way through the piles of books to his desk. Did you ever see him yourself?"

"Only later in Broadmoor," replied Auckland. "I'd like you to describe in your own words exactly how he struck you at the time."

"Well," I resumed, "my first impression of him was the extreme whiteness of his face. One felt on looking at him that he never went out into the sun. He had the unhealthy look that a plant gets if you leave a flower-pot over it and keep the light and air from it. His hair was long and straight and a dirty grey. Another thing that impressed me was the smoothness of his skin. You know how sometimes a man looks as though he has never had any need to shave—attractive in a young man but quite repulsive in an old one—well, that's how he looked. He stood up as I approached, and I saw he was a fat man, not grotesquely so but sufficiently to suggest grossness. His lips particularly were full and fleshy.

"I was half afraid of my own temerity in having entered, but he seemed glad to see me and said in rather a high-pitched voice:

" 'Come in, my dear boy; this is a most pleasant surprise. What can I do for you?'

"I mumbled something about being interested in old books and wanting to look round, and he readily assented. Shambling round from pile to pile, he set himself deliberately to interest me. And the man was a fascinating talker—in a very little while he had summed up my small stock of bibliographical knowledge and was enlightening me on dates, editions, issues, values, and other points of interest. It was with real regret that I glanced at my watch and found that I had to hurry back to school. I had made no purchase, but he insisted on presenting me with a book, a nicely bound copy of Sterne's *Sentimental Journey,* and made me promise to visit him again as soon as I could."

"Have you still got the Sterne?" asked Auckland.

"No," I said, "my father destroyed it at the time of the trial.

"As the shop was in a part of the town that was strictly out of bounds, I didn't mention my visit to my housemaster, but on the following Thursday it was too wet for cricket and I returned to my newly found friend.

"This time he took me up to a room on the first floor, where there were more books and several portfolios of prints. Race, for such I discovered was his name, was a mine of information on the political history of the eighteenth century, and kept me enthralled by his exposition of a great volume of Gillray cartoons. The man had a sort of magnetism, and at that impressionable age I fell completely under his spell. He drew me out about myself and my work at school, and it was impossible for a boy not to feel flattered by the attention of so learned a man. It was easy to forget his rather repellent physical qualities when he talked so brilliantly.

"Suddenly we heard the shop door below opening, and with an exclamation of annoyance he descended the stairs to attend to the customer. A minute or two passed, and he did not return. I listened and could hear the murmur of conversation below. I idly pulled a book or two from the shelves and glanced at them, but there was little in the room that he had not already shown me. I went to the door and peered down over the stairs, but couldn't see what was going on. My ears caught a scrap of dialogue about the county histories of Somerset. I became bored.

"Across the landing at the top of the stairs was another room, the door of which was very slightly ajar. I'm afraid that I'm of a very inquisitive disposition. I pushed it open and peeped in. It was obviously where Race lived. There was a bed in one corner, a wardrobe, and a circular table in the middle of the room, but what caught my eye at once and held me spellbound was a picture over the fireplace. No words of mine can describe it."

Auckland nodded. "I saw it—an unrecorded Goya—in his most bloodcurdling vein—made his 'Witches' Sabbath' look like a school treat! It was burned by our unimaginative police force. They wouldn't even let me photograph it." He sighed.

I resumed. "I went nearer to have a look at it. On the

mantelpiece below it was a book—the book you've got now on
your top shelf. I opened it and read the title page. Of course
it meant nothing to me. Gille de Retz doesn't feature in the
average school curriculum. Suddenly I heard a noise behind
me and swung round. There was Race standing in the doorway. He had come up the stairs without my hearing him. I
shall never forget the blazing fury in his eyes. His face
seemed whiter than ever as he stood there, a terrifying figure
literally shaking with rage.

"I quickly tried to make my apologies, but he silenced me
with a gesture; then he snatched the book from my hands and
replaced it on the mantelpiece. Still without speaking, he
pointed to the door and I went quickly down the stairs. He
followed me down into the shop. I was about to leave without
another word when suddenly his whole manner changed. It
was as though he had recollected some powerful reason for
conciliating me. He laid a hand on my arm.

" 'My dear boy,' he said, 'you must forgive my momentary
annoyance. I am a methodical man, and I can't bear people
touching the things in my room. I'm afraid that living as
something of a recluse has made me rather fussy. I quite
realise that you meant no harm. There are some very valuable books and pictures in there—not for sale, but my own
private collection, and naturally I can't allow customers to
wander in and out of it in my absence.'

"I expressed my contrition awkwardly enough, for the
whole situation had embarrassed me horribly and I felt ill at
ease. He perceived this and added:

" 'Now you mustn't worry about this—and least of all must
you let it stop you coming here. I want you to promise that
you'll visit me as soon as you can again—just to show that you
bear no ill-will. I'll hunt out some interesting things for you
to look at.'

"I gave him my promise and hurried back to school. In a
day or two I had persuaded myself that I'd been imagining
things, that some trick of the light had made him appear so
distorted with rage. After all, why should a man get so angry
about so little? As for the picture, it made comparatively

little impression on my schoolboy mind. Much that it depicted was unintelligible to me at that time. I was, in any case, unlikely to be invited into the private room again. And so I resolved to pay a further visit to the shop.

"An opportunity didn't occur for nearly a fortnight, and when I did manage to slip down to Bristol, there was no mistaking how glad he was to see me. He was almost gushing in his manner. He had been as good as his word in finding more books to show me, and I spent a most pleasant afternoon. Race was as voluble as ever, but I got the impression that he was slightly distrait, as though he were labouring under some sort of suppressed excitement. Several times as I looked up from a book I caught him looking at me in a queer reflective way, which made me feel a little uncomfortable. When I finally said that I must go, he made a suggestion that he had never made before.

" 'You've got very dusty,' he said. 'You really must wash your hands before you go. There's a basin downstairs—I'll turn on the light for you.'

"As he said this, he stepped across the shop, opened a door and turned a switch, illuminating a long flight of stairs. I descended them. They were of stone and led apparently into a cellar. As I reached the bottom step the light was extinguished. I turned sharply and saw him standing at the head of the stairs—a fantastic, foreshortened figure at the top of the shaft, silhouetted in the doorway. He had his hands stretched out, holding on to the jambs of the door, and with the half-light of the shop behind him he looked like a misshapen travesty of a cross. I called out to him and started to remount the stairs, but as I did so he quickly closed the door without saying a word.

"I was terribly afraid. Of course, it might have been a joke but I knew inside me that it wasn't and that I was in the most deadly peril. I reached the top of the stairs and groped at the door, but there seemed to be no handle inside. I couldn't find the switch either, it must have been in the shop. I shouted, there was no reply. An awful horror gripped me—the dank smell of the stone cellar, the lack of air, and the darkness, all conspired to undermine what little courage I possessed. I shouted again; then listened, holding my breath. All at once I heard the outer shop door open and an unfamiliar footstep inside the shop. With all my strength I pounded on the door, shouting and screaming like a madman. The noise reverberating round the confined space nearly deafened me. I listened again for a second; voices were raised in the shop, but I caught no words. I shouted again until I felt my lungs would burst and hammered on the door until my fists were bruised. Suddenly it was flung open and I stumbled out, hysterical with fear and half-blinded by the daylight. Before me stood an old clergyman, behind him Race, who bore on his face the same look of malevolent fury that I had seen before.

" 'What is the matter?" asked the clergyman. 'How did you get shut in there?'

"It was then that I made my fatal mistake. All I wanted was to get away and never come back again. If I lodged a complaint I foresaw endless trouble, with the school authorities, even with the police. My terror had evaporated with the daylight, and I was feeling more than a little ashamed of myself.

" 'I went down to wash my hands,' I said. 'The lights went out and I got frightened. I'm quite all right now, though.'

"The clergyman looked enquiringly at Race, but the latter had recovered his self-possession.

" 'The lights must have fused,' he said; 'they often do—it's the damp. I was just going to let him out when you came in. No wonder he was frightened. It's a most eerie place in the dark.'

"The clergyman looked from him to me, as if inviting some comment from me, but I merely said, 'I ought to be getting back to school now.'

"We left the shop together, and as we walked through the passage out of the court I looked back, and there was Race standing on the step of his shop following us with baleful eyes. My companion seemed to be debating whether he would ask me a question, but he refrained. I hardly liked to ask him to say nothing about the episode; he obviously wished to satisfy his curiosity, but we were complete strangers and, though old enough to be my grandfather, he seemed to be a diffident man. It was a curious relationship.

"He put me on to a bus, and I thanked him gravely. As we shook hands he said abruptly, 'I shouldn't go there again,' and turned away.

"For a few days I was on tenterhooks lest he should make any report of the occurrence to the school, but as the days became weeks and I heard no more, my mind became at rest. I had firmly decided that nothing would induce me to visit Race's shop again, and soon the whole episode assumed an air of unreality in my mind."

I looked at my watch.

"Good Lord!" I said to Auckland, "it's getting pretty late. Do you want to go to bed? We could have another session tomorrow."

"Certainly not," he replied. "I find your story of the most absorbing interest. It fills in all sorts of gaps in my knowledge of the affair. If you don't mind sitting up, I should greatly appreciate it if you'd carry on."

He refilled my glass and I settled myself more comfortably into my chair.

"Well," I continued, "I'm a bit diffident about telling the rest of the story. Up to now it's been pretty strange, but it has been sober fact; now we get into realms where I find myself a bit out of my depth."

Auckland nodded. "Never mind," he said, "let's have it. Just as it comes back to you—don't try to explain it, just tell me what happened."

"A year passed and I was still at school," I continued; "I'd got into the Sixth Form and was working pretty hard for a scholarship. I'd also got into the House Cricket XI by some miracle, and so I couldn't be so free-and-easy about games as I had been previously. Public opinion forced me to take them fairly seriously. A dropped catch at a critical point in a match can make a schoolboy's life pretty good hell.

"At that age I used to sleep extraordinarily well—I still do for that matter. It was very rare for me to dream and then only of trivial affairs. But on the night of June 26th—I noted the date in my diary—I had the first of a couple of particularly horrible dreams. I dreamed most vividly that I was back in Race's shop. Every detail of that untidy interior passed in an accurate picture through my brain. I was standing in the middle of the shop, and it was dusk. Very little light came through those dusty windows piled high with books. Race himself was nowhere to be seen. The door to the cellar, which had such sinister associations for me, was closed. Suddenly from the other side of it came a series of appalling screams and shouts, intermingled with muffled bangs and thumps on the door. I ran across and tried to open it, but it was locked. Then I darted out to the shop steps to see if anyone were at hand to assist me, but the court was deserted. I stood irresolute in the shop, and then all at once the cries seemed to get weaker and the banging on the door ceased. I listened and could hear the sounds of a struggle on the stairs gradually getting fainter as it reached the cellar below.

"At this point I awoke shivering with fright, bathed in a cold sweat. Sleep was impossible for me during the rest of the night. I lay and thought about my dream. It seemed so queer that I should dream, not of my own experience on the stairs, but from the point of view of an observer.

"The next night exactly the same thing occurred, and the horror of the scene so impressed me that I must have cried out in my sleep, for I found that I'd awakened several of the other boys in my dormitory. I couldn't bear the anticipation of having such a dream a third time, and I went to the House Matron on the following day and told her that I couldn't sleep. She moved me from the dormitory into the sick-room and gave me a sedative. On that night and thereafter I slept quite normally again.

"Not quite a fortnight later a further link was forged in this extraordinary chain of events. I was passing the local police-station and I stopped to read a notice posted outside about the protection of wild birds—I've always been a bit of an ornithologist. Along the railings in front of the building were hung the usual medley of notices—Lost, Found, and

Missing. My eye caught one more recent than the others—and I idly read it.

"I cannot, of course, remember the exact wording at this date, but it asked for information about a boy named Roger Weyland, aged fifteen and a half. He was described in detail, and I remember being struck at once by his similarity to myself. He had left his home at Clevedon after lunch on June 26th to bicycle into Bristol, where he intended to visit the docks. He was last seen near St. Mary Redcliffe at about half-past five the same afternoon, and the police were asking anyone to come forward who could throw light on his whereabouts.

"I read and reread the notice. Its implication dawned on me at once. It's no good asking why, but I assure you that at the moment I *knew* what had happened. My dream of the night of June 26th was still fresh in my memory, and even in the broad sunlit street I shuddered and was oppressed by a feeling of nameless horror.

"I debated what I should do. The police, I felt sure, would laugh at me. I could never bring myself to walk into the station and blurt out such a fantastic tale to some grinning sergeant. But I must tell someone; and after dinner that day I sought an interview with my housemaster. He was a most understanding man, and listened in patient silence while I told him the whole story. I must have spoken with conviction, because at the end of it he rang up a friend of his, a local Inspector of Police. Half an hour later I repeated my tale to him. He was very polite, asked one or two searching questions, but I could see that he was sceptical. He did, however, agree with my housemaster that Race's activities might profitably be looked into.

"If you followed the trial, I suppose you know all the rest—how they found the boy's body and God-knows-what other devilish things beside. My name was suppressed in the evidence, and I left school at the end of that term and went abroad for six months.

"One very odd thing about it all was that they never traced the clergyman. The police were most anxious to get him to corroborate my story, and my father was equally keen to find him—after all, he saved my life—and my father wanted to show some tangible appreciation of the fact, subscribe generously to one of his favourite charities or something. It's very queer really that the police, with all their nation-wide organisation, never got on to him. After all, there aren't a limitless number of clergymen, and the number of those in the Bristol area that afternoon must have been comparatively small. Perhaps he didn't like to come forward and be connected with such a business, but I don't think that's very likely—he didn't strike me as the sort of man who would shirk his obligations.

"That's really all that I can tell you, and I expect you knew some of that already."

"A certain amount," replied Auckland, "but by no means all. I occasionally get asked questions by the police in this kind of case, and I did assist them on this occasion, though I wasn't called in evidence. Race had a damned good counsel in Rutherford, and managed to convince the jury that he was insane. If a man is sufficiently wicked, a British jury will often believe that he must be mad. And so he went to Broadmoor. Of course, he was as sane as you and I are."

"How did you come to get hold of one of his books?" I asked.

"Through the good offices of the police," he said. "Perhaps as a sort of consolation prize for my distress at the destruction of the Goya. The book is really the clue to Race.

"It is a contemporary account of the activities of Gille de Retz, Marshal of France, hanged at Nantes in 1440. I expect you know a certain amount about him; he figures in all the standard works on Diabolism. The contemporary authorities are a bit vague on the exact number of children he murdered—Monstrelet says a hundred and sixty, but Chastellain and some others put it at a hundred and forty. But all this is general knowledge.

"What isn't so widely known is that every now and then he seems to reappear in history—at least the devilish practices, with which his name is associated, crop up again and again.

He was quite a cult in seventeenth-century Venice, and there was a case in Bohemia in the middle of the last century. A variant of de Retz's name is de Rais, and Race himself claimed to be a descendant; but I've no proof of this. The police failed to trace his parentage or to find any details about him before he appeared in Bristol just before the First World War. His shop has gone now; the whole of that area was pulled down in a recent slum-clearance scheme.

"The trial at Nantes in 1440 has always been an interest of mine, and I had a great find the last time I was in Paris. Some early Nantes archives had recently been acquired by the Bibliothèque Nationale, and I spent a happy week examining all the original documents relating to the examination of the woman, La Meffrie, who procured most of the children for de Retz. I've got transcripts of the most important. Would you care to borrow them? They are quite enthralling."

"Not on your life," I replied as I rose to take my leave. "I came far too near to playing the principal role to read about such things with any pleasure. *You* may be able to take a detached, scientific view of the case, but, believe me, I've had enough of de Retz and all his works to last me a lifetime."

THE FIRST SHEAF

H. R. Wakefield

"IF ONLY they realized what they were doing!" laughed old Porteous, leaning over the side of the car. "They" were a clutter of rustics, cuddling vegetable marrows, cauliflowers, apples, and other stuffs, passing into a village church some miles south of Birmingham. "Humanity has been doing that, performing that rite, since thousands of years before the first syllable of recorded time, I suppose; though not always in quite such a refined manner. And then there are maypoles, of all indecorous symbols, and beating the bounds, a particularly interesting survival with, originally, a dual function; first they beat the bounds to scare the devils out, and then they beat the small boys that their tears might propitiate the Rain Goddess. Such propitiation having been found to be superfluous in this climate, they have ceased to beat the urchins; a great pity, but an admirable example of myth-adaptation. Great Britain swarms with such survivals, some as innocuous and bland as this harvest festival, others far more formidable and guarded secrets; at least that was so when I was a boy. Did I ever tell you how I lost my arm?"

"No," I replied, yawning. "Go ahead. But I hope the tale has entertainment value, for I am feeling deliciously sleepy."

Old Porteous leaned back and lit a cigar. He had started his career with fifty pounds, and turned this into seven figures by sheer speculative genius; he seemed to touch nothing which did not appreciate. He is fat, shrewd, cynical, and very charitable in an individual, far-sighted way. A copious but discriminating eater and drinker, to all appearances just a superb epitome of a type. But he has a less mundane side which is highly developed, being a devoted amateur of music with a trained and individual taste. And he owns the finest collection of keyboard instruments in Europe, the only one of his many possessions I very greatly envy him. Music, indeed, was the cause of our being together that Sunday morning in August, for I make my living out of attempting to criticise it, and we were driving to Manchester for a Harty Sibelius concert.

When I was a boy of thirteen [he began] my father accepted the living of Reedley End in Essex. There was little competition for the curé as the place had a notable reputation for toughness in the diocese, and the stipend was two hundred and fifty pounds a year and a house which, in size and amenities, somewhat resembled a contemporary poor-house. However, the prospect appealed to my dear old dad's zeal, for he was an Evangelist by label and temperament.

Reedley End was in one of those remote corners of the country which are "backwaterish" to this day; and was then almost as cut off from the world as a village in Tibet. It sprawled along the lower slopes of a short, narrow valley, was fifteen miles from a railway station, and its only avenue to anywhere was a glorified cart-track. It was peopled by a strange tribe, aloof, dour, bitter, and revealing copious signs of intensive interbreeding. They greeted my father's arrival with contemptuous nonchalance, spurned his ministrations, and soon enough broke his spirit.

"I can do nothing with them!" he groaned, half to himself and half to me. "They seem to worship other gods than mine!"

There was a very real justification for their bitterness. Reedley End was, perhaps, the most arid spot in Britain; drought, save in very good years, was endemic in that part of Essex, and I believe a bad spring and dry summer still causes great inconvenience and some hardship to this day. There had been three successive drought years before our arrival, with crop failures, heavy mortality amongst the beasts, and actual thirst the result. The distress was great and growing, and a mood of venomous despair had come with it. There was no one to help them—the day of Governmental paternalism had not yet dawned, and my father's predecessor's prayers for rain had been a singularly ineffectual substitute. They were off the map and left to stew in their own juice—or rather perish from the lack of it. Men in such a pass, if they cannot look forward for succour, many times look back.

In February they went forth to sow again, and my father told me they seemed to him in a sinister and enigmatic mood. (I may say my mother had died five years before, I was an only child, and through being my father's confidant, was old and "wise" for my age.) Their habitual aloofness had become impenetrable, and all—even the children—seemed imbued with some communal purpose, sharers of some communal secret.

One morning my father went to visit an ancient, bed-ridden crone who snubbed him with less consistent ruthlessness than the rest of his fearsome flock. To his astonishment he found the village entirely deserted. When he entered the ancient's cottage she abruptly told him to be gone.

"It is no day for you to be abroad, parson," she said peremptorily. "Go home and stay indoors!"

In his bewilderment my father attempted to solve the humiliating mystery, and decided to visit one of the three small farmers who strove desperately to scrape a living for themselves and their hinds from the parched acres; and who had treated him with rough courtesy. His farmhouse was some two miles away and my father set out to walk there. But, on reaching the outskirts of the village, he found his way barred by three men placed like sentries across the track. They waved him back without a word, and when he made some show of passing them, grew so threatening and their gestures were so unmistakable that my father cut short his protests and came miserably home again.

That night I couldn't sleep; my father's disturbed mood

had communicated itself to me. Some time in the course of it I went to my window and leaned out. A bitter northerly wind was blowing, and suddenly down it came a horrid, thin cry of agony that seemed to have been carried from afar. It came once again, diminished and cut short. I crept shivering and badly scared back to bed.

If my father had heard it he made no reference to it next morning, when the village seemed itself again. And though the children were brooding and subdued, their elders were almost in good spirits, ruthlessly jocund, like homing lynchers. (I made that comparison, of course, long afterwards, but I know it to be psychologically true.)

My father had made valiant and pathetic attempts to get hold of the village youth and managed to coax together a meagre attendance at a Sunday school. On the next Sunday one of the dozen was missing. This was a girl of about my own age, the only child of a farm-labourer and his wife. He was a "foreigner," a native of Sussex, and a sparklingly hand-some fellow of the pure Saxon type. His wife had some claims to be a beauty, too, and was much fairer than the average of those parts. The result was an oddly lovely child, as fair and rosy as her father. She shone out in the village like a Golden Oriole in a crew of crows. She aroused my keenest curiosity, the bud of love, I suppose; and I spent much of my time spying on her from a shy distance. When she failed to turn up that Sunday, my father went round to her parents' cottage. They were both at home. The man was pacing up and down the kitchen, his face revealing fury and grief. The mother was sitting in front of the fire, wearing an expression my father found it hard to analyse. It reminded him of the appearance often shown by religious maniacs in their less boisterous moments; ecstatic, exalted, yet essentially unbalanced. When he asked after the little girl, the father clenched his fists and swore fiercely, the woman, without turning her head, mut-tered, "She'll be coming to school no more." This ultimatum was naturally not good enough for my father, who was disagreeably affected by the scene. He asked where she was. She'd been sent away. "Where to?" he asked. But at this she became a raging virago and ordered my father to go and mind his own business. He turned to the man, who seemed on the verge of an outburst, but she muttered something my father couldn't catch and he ran from the room.

Late that night my dad heard a tap on his study window. It was the father.

"Sir," he said, "I'm away. They're devils here!"

"Your little girl?" asked my father, horrified.

"They've taken her," he replied hoarsely. "I don't know why, and I don't know where she's gone. But I know I shan't see her no more. As for my wife, I hate her for what she's done. She says they'll kill me if I try to find her. They'd kill me if they knew I was here!"

My father implored him to tell him more; promised him sanctuary and protection, but all he said was, "Avenge her, sir!" and vanished into the night.

Naturally my father was at a loss what to do. He even enlisted my more than willing aid. But all I succeeded in doing was verifying the agonising fact that my darling had gone, and in taking a terrific beating from persons unknown one night when I was snooping near the cottage.

In the end my father wrote a confidential letter to the Colchester police outlining the circumstances. But I suppose his tale was so vague and discreet that, though some enquiries were made by a thick-skulled, pot-bellied constable, nothing whatsoever came of them. But my father was a marked man from the moment of this peeler's appearance, and audible and impertinent interruptions punctuated his services.

Realising he was beaten, he made up his mind, with many tears and self-reproaches, to resign at the end of the year.

The week after the little girl's disappearance there was a lovely two days' rain, and the spring and summer were a farmer's Elysian dream. My father, with pathetic optimism, hoped this copious, if belated, answer to his prayers would improve his status with his iron-fleeced flock. Instead he experienced an unanimous and shattering ostracism. In despair he wrote to his bishop, but the episcopal counsel was couched in too general and booming terms to be efficacious in converting the denizens of Reedley End.

And one day it was August, the fields shone with a mighty harvest, and it was time to bring it home.

The valley divided the corn-lands of Reedley into two areas tilled against the slight slopes. Those facing north were noticeably less productive than those on the south and do not concern us. Those southern fields were open and treeless, with one exception, a comparatively small circular field in the very middle of the tilled expanse. This was completely hemmed in by evergreens, yews, and holm-oaks, not a single deciduous tree interrupted the dark barrier. In the centre of this field was a stone pillar about eight feet high. I was forced to be by myself for many hours a day; and I spent many of them roaming the country-side and peopling it with the folk of my fancy. The local youth regarded me without enthusiasm, but young blood is thicker than old and they did not keep me in rigid "Coventry," though they were very guarded in their replies to my questions.

This circular field stirred an intense curiosity within me, and all my wanderings on the southern slopes seemed to bring me, sooner or later, to its boundaries. Eventually I summoned up courage to ask a lad who had shown traces of cordiality if the field had a name—for some reason I was sure it had. He looked at me oddly—nervously and angrily—and replied, "It's the Good Field; and nought to do with you!" After the little girl's disappearance I was convinced, vaguely but certainly, that this field was concerned with it; intuition I suppose.

"Now that," I interrupted, "is a word that baffles me; and the dictionary seems to know no more than I do."

In a way I agree [laughed old Porteous], I could answer you negatively and quite accurately by saying that it is a mode of apprehension unknown to women. But I believe an intuitive judgment to be a syllogism of which the premises are in the

Unconscious, the conclusion in the Conscious, though retrospective meditation can sometimes resolve it into a normal thought process. I have often done so in the case of big deals. It is the speed of the intuitive process which is so valuable. And now I hope you are a wiser man!

Anyway I conceived a fascinated horror of the field, a shivering curiosity concerning it I longed to satisfy.

One evening, early in March, I determined to do what I had never dared before, walk out into the field and examine the stone pillar. It was almost dusk and not a soul in sight. When I'd surmounted a small but deep ditch, broken through between two yews, and stood out in that strange place under a hurrying, unstable sky, I felt a sense of extreme isolation; not, I think, the isolation of being alone in a deserted place, but such as one would experience if alone and horribly conspicuous amongst a hostile crowd. However, I fought down my fears and strode forward. When I reached the pillar I found it was square and surrounded by a small, cleared expanse of neatly tiled stone. This stone was thickly stained with what appeared to be red rust. The pillar itself was heavily pitted and indented about a third from its top, with such regularity as suggested an almost obliterated inscription of some kind. I clasped the pillar with my arms, tucked my legs round it, and heaved myself up till I could touch its top. This I found to be hollowed out into a cup. I stretched up farther and pushed my fingers down. The next moment I was lying on my back and wringing my fingers; for if I had dipped my hand into molten lead I couldn't have known a sharper scald. This emptied my little bag of courage and, with "zero at the bone," I got up and ran for it. As I stumbled forward I took one look over my shoulder, and it seemed to me there was a dark figure standing by the pillar and reaching high above its top; and all the time I gasped homewards I felt I had a follower, and the pursuit was not called off till I flung myself through the rectory door.

"What's the matter?" asked my father. "You shouldn't run like that. And you've cut your hand. Go and bathe it."

They started to reap in the second week of August and I found the process of great interest, for it was the first harvest I had seen. I hovered about the outskirts of the activity, fearing my reception if I ventured nearer. I found they were working in towards the Round Field from all points of the compass; and, young and inexperienced as I was, it seemed to me the people were in a strange mood, or rather mood-cycle, for at times there would be outbursts of wild singing, with horse-play and gesticulation, and at others they would be even more morose and silent than had been their sombre wont. And day after day they drew nearer the Round Field.

They reached it from all sides almost simultaneously by about noon on a superbly fine day. And then to my astonishment, they all stopped work and went home. That was on a Tuesday, and they did nothing the next day in the fields, though they were anything but idle. There was incessant activity in the village of a sort which perplexed my father greatly. It struck him that something of great importance was being prepared. The hive was seething. Needless to say no knowledge of it was vouchsafed to him. He discovered by humiliating experience that a meeting of the older men was held in what was known as "Odiues Field," for the sentries posted round all the approaches to it brusquely and menacingly refused him entrance.

Now whether it was our old friend, Intuition, or not, I was convinced these plans and consultations concerned the Round Field, and that something was due to be done there on the morrow. So I crept out of the house an hour before dawn, leaving a note on the hall-table telling my father not to worry. I took with me three slices of bread-and-butter and a bottle of water. I made my way to the Round Field by a devious route so as to avoid passing through the village, creeping along the hedgerows and keeping a sharp look-out with eye and ear. I have said that a ditch encircled the field, and in it I crouched down between two yews, well away from the gates. By creeping into the space where their branches touched, I believed I could spy out undetected.

Dawn broke fine, but very heavy and close, and there were red strata of clouds to the east as the sun climbed through them.

To my surprise no one appeared at six, their usual hour for starting work, nor at seven, eight, or nine, when I ate half my bread-and-butter and sipped the bottle. By ten o'clock I had made up my mind that nothing would happen and I'd better go home, when I heard voices in the field behind me and knew it was too late to retreat if I'd wanted to. I could see nothing ahead of me save the high, white wheat, but presently I heard more voices and two men with sickles came cutting their way past me, and soon I could see an arc of a ring of them slashing towards the centre. When they had advanced some fifty yards I had a better view to right and left, and a very strange sight I beheld. The villagers, mostly old people and children, were streaming through the gates. All were clad in black with wreaths of corn around their necks. They formed in line behind the reapers and moved slowly forward. They made no sound—I heard not a single child's cry—but stared in a rapt way straight before them. Slowly and steadily the reapers cut their way forward. By this time the sun had disappeared and a dense cloud-bank was spreading from the east. By four o'clock the reapers had met in the centre round the last small patch of wheat by the stone pillar. And there they stopped, laid down their sickles, and took their stand in front of the people. For, perhaps, five minutes they all stayed motionless with bowed heads. And then they lifted their faces to the sky and began to chant. And a very odd song they sang, one which made me shiver beneath the yew branches. It was mainly in the minor mode, but at perfectly regular intervals it transposed into the major in a tremendous, but perfectly controlled, cry of exaltation and ecstacy. I have heard nothing like it since, though a "Spiritual," sung by four thousand god-drunk darkies in Georgia, faintly reminded me of it. But this was something far more formidable, far more primitive; in fact it seemed like the oldest song ever sung. The last, fierce, sustained shout of triumph made me tremble with some unnameable emotion, and I longed to be out there shouting with them. When it ended they all knelt down save one old, white-bearded man with a wreath of corn around his brow who, taking some of the corn in his right hand, raised it above his head and stared into the sky. At once four men came forward and, with what seemed like large trowels, began digging with them. The people then rose to their feet, somewhat obstructing my view. But soon the four men had finished their work and stood upright. Then the old man stepped out again and I could see he was holding what appeared to be a short iron bar. With this he pounded the earth for some moments. Then, picking up something, it looked as if he dropped it into a vessel, a dark, metal pot, I fancied, and paced to the stone pillar, raised his right arm and poured the contents into the cup at the pillar's top. At that moment a terrific flash of lightning cut down from the clouds and enveloped the pillar in mauve and devilish flame; and there came such a piercing blast of thunder that I fell backwards into the ditch. When I'd struggled back, the rain was hurling itself down in such fury that it was bouncing high off the lanes of stiff soil. Dimly through it I could see that all the folk had prostrated themselves once more. But in two minutes the thunder-cloud had run with the squall and the sun was blazing from a clear sky. The four men then bound up the corn in that last patch and placed the sheaf in front of the pillar. After which the old man, leading the people, paced the length of the field, scattering something from the vessel in the manner of one sowing. And he led them out of the gate and that was the last I saw of them.

Now somehow I felt that if they knew I'd been watching them, it would have gone hard with me. So I determined to wait for dusk. I was stiff, cold, and hungry, but I stuck it till the sun went flaming down and the loveliest after-glow I ever remember had faded. While I waited there a resolve had been forming in my mind. I had the most intense desire to know what the old man had dropped in the hollow on the pillar, and curiosity is in all animals the strongest foe of fear. Every moment that emotion grew more compelling, and

when at last it was just not dark it became over-mastering. I
stumbled across as fast as I could to the pillar, looking neither
to right nor left, clambered up and thrust down my hand. I
could feel small pieces of what might have been wood, and
then it was as if my forefinger was caught and gripped. The
most agonising pain shot up my arm and through my body. I
fell to the ground and shook my hand wildly to free my
finger from that which held it. In the end it clattered down
beside me and splintered on the stone. And then the blood
streamed from my finger, which had been punctured to the
bone. Somehow I struggled home leaving a trail of blood
behind me.

The next day my arm was swollen up like a black bladder,
the morning after it was amputated at the shoulder. The
surgeon who operated on me came up to my father in the
hospital and held something out to him. "I found this em-
bedded in your son's finger," he said.

"What is it?" asked my father.

"A child's tooth," he replied. "I suppose he's been fighting
someone, someone with a very dirty mouth!"

"And that's why," said old Porteous, "though I have none
of my own, I have ever since shown the greatest respect to the
gods of others."

VENGEFUL SPIRITS

The ghost who returns to collect payment for death or for some old wrong is also a common visitant. But when that payment falls upon the innocent bystander, the results are more horrifying and frightening. For—with a little imagination—the reader can be one with the victim.

HOW FEAR DEPARTED
FROM THE LONG GALLERY

E. F. Benson

CHURCH-PEVERIL is a house so beset and frequented by spectres, both visible and audible, that none of the family which it shelters under its acre and a half of green copper roofs takes psychical phenomena with any seriousness. For to the Peverils the appearance of a ghost is a matter of hardly greater significance than the appearance of the post to those who live in more ordinary houses. It arrives, that is to say, practically every day, it knocks (or makes other noises), it is observed coming up the drive (or in other places). I myself, when staying there, have seen the present Mrs. Peveril, who is rather short-sighted, peer into the dusk, while we were taking our coffee on the terrace after dinner, and say to her daughter:

"My dear, was not that the Blue Lady who has just gone into the shrubbery? I hope she won't frighten Flo. Whistle for Flo, dear."

(Flo, it may be remarked, is the youngest and most precious of many dachshunds.)

Blanche Peveril gave a cursory whistle, and crunched the sugar left unmelted at the bottom of her coffee-cup between her very white teeth.

"Oh, darling, Flo isn't so silly as to mind," she said. "Poor blue Aunt Barbara is such a bore! Whenever I meet her she always looks as if she wanted to speak to me, but when I say, 'What is it, Aunt Barbara?' she never speaks, but only points

somewhere toward the house, which is so vague. I believe
there was something she wanted to confess about two hundred years ago, but she has forgotten what it is."

Here Flo gave two or three short pleased barks, and came
out of the shrubbery wagging her tail, and capering round
what appeared to me to be a perfectly empty space on the
lawn.

"There! Flo has made friends with her," said Mrs. Peveril.
"I wonder why she dresses in that very stupid shade of blue."

From this it may be gathered that even with regard to psychic
phenomena there is some truth in the proverb that speaks of
familiarity. But the Peverils do not exactly treat their ghosts
with contempt, since most of that delightful family never
despised anybody except such people as avowedly did not
care for hunting or shooting, or golf or skating. And as all of
their ghosts are of their family, it seems reasonable to suppose
that they all, even the poor Blue Lady, excelled at one time
in field-sports. So far then they harbor no such unkindness or
contempt, but only pity. Of one Peveril, indeed, who broke
his neck in vainly attempting to ride up the main staircase on
a thoroughbred mare after some monstrous and violent deed
in the back-garden, they are very fond, and Blanche comes
downstairs in the morning with an eye unusually bright
when she can announce that Master Anthony was "very
loud" last night. He (apart from the fact of his having been
so foul a ruffian) was a tremendous fellow across country, and
they like these indications of the continuance of his superb
vitality. In fact, it is supposed to be a compliment, when you
go to stay at Church-Peveril, to be assigned a bedroom which
is frequented by defunct members of the family. It means
that you are worthy to look on the august and villainous
dead, and you will find yourself shown into some vaulted or
tapestried chamber, without benefit of electric light, and are
told that great-great-grandmamma Bridget occasionally has
vague business by the fireplace, but it is better not to talk to
her, and that you will hear Master Anthony "awfully well" if
he attempts the front staircase any time before morning.

There you are left for your night's repose, and, having quakingly undressed, begin reluctantly to put out your candles. It is draughty in these great chambers, and the solemn tapestry swings and bellows and subsides, and the fire-light dances on the forms of huntsmen and warriors and stern pursuits. Then you climb into your bed, a bed so huge that you feel as if the desert of Sahara was spread for you, and pray, like the mariners who sailed with St. Paul, for day. And, all the time, you are aware that Freddy and Harry and Blanche and possibly even Mrs. Peveril are quite capable of dressing up and making disquieting tappings outside your door, so that when you open it some inconjecturable horror fronts you. For myself, I stick steadily to the assertion that I have an obscure valvular disease of the heart, and so sleep undisturbed in the new wing of the house, where Aunt Barbara and great-great-grandmamma Bridget and Master Anthony never penetrate. I forget the details of great-great-grandmamma Bridget, but she certainly cut the throat of some distant relation before she disembowelled herself with the axe that had been used at Agincourt. Before that she had led a very sultry life, crammed with amazing incidents.

But there is one ghost at Church-Peveril at which the family never laugh, in which they feel no friendly and amused interest, and of which they only speak just as much as is necessary for the safety of their ghosts. More properly it should be described as two ghosts, for the "haunt" in question is that of two very young children, who were twins. These, not without reason, the family take very seriously indeed. The story of them, as told me by Mrs. Peveril, is as follows:

In the year 1602, the same being the last of Queen Elizabeth's reign, a certain Dick Peveril was greatly in favor at Court. He was brother to Master Joseph Peveril, then owner of the family house and lands, who two years previously, at the respectable age of seventy-four, became father of twin-boys, first-born of his progeny. It is known that the royal and ancient virgin had said to handsome Dick, who was nearly forty years his brother's junior, " 'Tis pity that you are not

master of Church-Peveril," and these words probably suggested to him a sinister design. Be that as it may, handsome
Dick, who very adequately sustained the family reputation
for wickedness, set off to ride down to Yorkshire, and found
that, very conveniently, his brother Joseph had just been
seized with an apoplexy, which appeared to be the result of a
continued spell of hot weather combined with the necessity
of quenching his thirst with an augmented amount of sack,
and had actually died while handsome Dick, with God knows
what thoughts in his mind, was journeying northwards. Thus
it came about that he arrived at Church-Peveril just in time
for his brother's funeral. It was with great propriety that he
attended the obsequies, and returned to spend a sympathetic
day or two of mourning with his widowed sister-in-law, who
was but a faint-hearted dame, little fit to be mated with such
hawks as these. On the second night of his stay, he did that
which the Peverils regret to this day. He entered the room
where the twins slept with their nurse and quietly strangled
the latter as she slept. Then he took the twins and put them
into the fire which warms the long gallery. The weather,
which up to the day of Joseph's death had been so hot, had
changed suddenly to bitter cold, and the fire was heaped high
with burning logs and was exultant with flame. In the core of
this conflagration he struck out a cremation-chamber, and
into that he threw the two children, stamping them down
with his riding-boots. They could just walk, but they could
not walk out of that ardent place. It is said that he laughed as
he added more logs. Thus he became master of Church-
Peveril.

The crime was never brought home to him, but he lived
no longer than a year in the enjoyment of his blood-stained
inheritance. When he lay adying he made his confession to
the priest who attended him, but his spirit struggled forth
from its fleshly coil before Absolution could be given him.
On that very night there began in Church-Peveril the haunting which to this day is but seldom spoken of by the family,
and then only in low tones with serious mien. For, only an
hour or two after handsome Dick's death, one of the servants

passing the door of the long gallery heard from within peals
of the loud laughter so jovial and yet so sinister, which he had
thought would never be heard in the house again. In a
moment of that cold courage which is so nearly akin to
mortal terror, he opened the door and entered, expecting to
see he knew not what manifestation of him who lay dead in
the room below. Instead he saw two little white-robed figures
toddling towards him hand in hand across the moonlit floor.

The watchers in the room below ran upstairs startled by
the crash of his fallen body, and found him lying in the grip
of some dread convulsion. Just before morning he regained
consciousness and told his tale. Then pointing with trembling and ash-grey finger towards the door, he screamed
aloud, and so fell back dead.

During the next fifty years this strange and terrible legend of
the twin-babies became fixed and consolidated. Their appearance, luckily for those who inhabited the house, was
exceedingly rare, and during these years they seem to have
been seen four or five times only. On each occasion they
appeared at night, between sunset and sunrise, always in the
same long gallery, and always as two toddling children
scarcely able to walk. And on each occasion the luckless
individual who saw them died either speedily or terribly, or
with both speed and terror, after the accursed vision had
appeared to him. Sometimes he might live for a few months:
he was lucky if he died, as did the servant who first saw them,
in a few hours. Vastly more awful was the fate of a certain
Mrs. Canning, who had the ill-luck to see them in the middle
of the next century, or to be quite accurate, in the year 1760.
By this time the hours and the place of their appearance were
well known, and, as up till a year ago, visitors were warned
not to go between sunset and sunrise into the long gallery.

But Mrs. Canning, a brilliantly clever and beautiful woman,
admirer also and friend of the notorious sceptic M. Voltaire,
wilfully went and sat night after night in spite of all pro-
testations, in the haunted place. For four evenings she saw
nothing, but on the fifth she had her will, for the door in the

middle of the gallery opened, and there came toddling towards her the ill-omened, innocent little pair. It seemed that
even then she was not frightened, but she thought good, poor
wretch, to mock at them, telling them it was time for them to
get back into the fire. They gave no word in answer, but
turned away from her, crying and sobbing. Immediately after
they disappeared from her vision and she rustled downstairs
to where the family and guests in the house were waiting for
her, with the triumphant announcement that she had seen
them both, and must needs write to M. Voltaire, saying that
she had spoken to spirits made manifest. It would make him
laugh. But when some months later the whole news reached
him he did not laugh at all.

Mrs. Canning was one of the great beauties of her day, and
in the year 1760 she was at the height and zenith of her
blossoming. The chief beauty, if it is possible to single out
one point where all was so exquisite, lay in the dazzling color
and incomparable brilliance of her complexion. She was now
just thirty years of age, but in spite of the excesses of her life,
retained the snow and roses of girlhood, and she courted the
bright light of day which other women shunned, for it but
showed to greater advantage the splendor of her skin. In
consequence she was very considerably dismayed one morning, about a fortnight after her strange experience in the long
gallery, to observe on her left cheek an inch or two below her
turquoise-colored eyes, a little greyish patch of skin, about as
big as a threepenny piece. It was in vain that she applied her
accustomed washes and unguents; vain, too, were the arts of
her *fardeuse* and of her medical adviser. For a week she kept
herself secluded, martyring herself with solitude and unaccustomed physics, and for result at the end of the week she
had no amelioration to comfort herself with: instead, this
woeful grey patch had doubled itself in size. Thereafter the
nameless disease, whatever it was, developed in new and
terrible ways. From the center of the discolored place there
sprouted forth little lichen-like tendrils of greenish-grey, and
another patch appeared on her lower lip. This, too, soon
vegetated, and one morning on opening her eyes to the

horror of the new day, she found that her vision was strangely
blurred. She sprang to her looking-glass, and what she saw
caused her to shriek aloud with horror. From under her
upper eyelid a fresh growth had sprung up, mushroom-like,
in the night, and its filaments extended downwards, screen-
ing the pupil of her eye. Soon after her tongue and throat
were attacked: the air passages became obstructed, and death
by suffocation was merciful after such suffering.

More terrible yet was the case of a certain Colonel Blantyre
who fired at the children with his revolver. What he went
through is not to be recorded here.

It is this haunting, then, that the Peverils take quite seriously, and every guest on his arrival in the house is told that
the long gallery must not be entered after nightfall on any
pretext whatever. By day, however, it is a delightful room
and intrinsically merits description, apart from the fact that
the due understanding of its geography is necessary for the
account that here follows. It is full eighty feet in length, and
is lit by a row of six tall windows looking over the gardens at
the back of the house. A door communicates with the landing
at the top of the main staircase, and about half-way down the
gallery in the wall facing the windows is another door com-
municating with the back staircase and servants' quarters,
and thus the gallery forms a constant place of passage for
them in going to the rooms on the first landing. It was
through this door that the baby-figures came when they
appeared to Mrs. Canning, and on several other occasions
they have been known to make their entry here, for the room
out of which handsome Dick took them lies just beyond at
the top of the back stairs. Further on again in the gallery is
the fireplace into which he thrust them, and at the far end a
large box-window looks straight down the avenue. Above this
fireplace, there hangs with grim significance a portrait of
handsome Dick, in the insolent beauty of early manhood,
attributed to Holbein, and a dozen other portraits of great
merit face the windows. During the day this is the most
frequented sitting-room in the house, for its other visitors

never appear there then, nor does it then ever resound with the harsh jovial laugh of handsome Dick, which sometimes, after dark has fallen, is heard by passers-by on the landing outside. But Blanche does not grow bright-eyed when she hears it: she shuts her ears and hastens to put a greater distance between her and the sound of that atrocious mirth.

But during the day the long gallery is frequented by many occupants, and much laughter in no wise sinister or saturnine resounds there. When summer lies hot over the land, those occupants lounge in the deep window-seats, and when winter spreads his icy fingers and blows shrilly between his frozen palms, congregate around the fireplace at the far end, and perch, in companies of cheerful chatterers, upon sofa and chair, and chair-back and floor. Often have I sat there on long August evenings up till dressing-time, but never have I been there when anyone has seemed disposed to linger over-late without hearing the warning: "It is close on sunset: shall we go?" Later on in the shorter autumn days they often have tea laid there, and sometimes it has happened that, even while merriment was most uproarious, Mrs. Peveril has suddenly looked out of the window and said, "My dears, it is getting so late: let us finish our nonsense downstairs in the hall." And then for a moment a curious hush always falls on loquacious family and guests alike, and as if some bad news had just been known, we all make our silent way out of the place. But the spirits of the Peverils (of the living ones, that is to say) are the most mercurial imaginable, and the blight which the thought of handsome Dick and his doings casts over them passes away again with amazing rapidity.

A typical party, large, young, and peculiarly cheerful, was staying at Church-Peveril shortly after Christmas last year, and as usual on December 31, Mrs. Peveril was giving her annual New Year's Eve ball. The house was quite full, and she had commandeered as well the greater part of the Peveril Arms to provide sleeping-quarters for the overflow from the house. For some days past a black and windless frost had stopped all hunting, but it is an ill windlessness that blows no good (if so mixed a metaphor may be forgiven) , and the lake below the house had for the last day or two been covered with an adequate and admirable sheet of ice. Everyone in the house had been occupied all the morning of that day in performing swift and violent manoeuvres on the elusive surface, and as soon as lunch was over we all, with one exception, hurried out again. This one exception was Madge Dalrymple, who had had the misfortune to fall rather badly earlier in the day, but hoped, by resting her injured knee, instead of joining the skaters again, to be able to dance that evening. The hope, it is true, was of the most sanguine sort, for she could but hobble ignobly back to the house, but with the breezy optimism which characterizes the Peverils (she is Blanche's first cousin) , she remarked that it would be but tepid enjoyment that she could, in her present state, derive from further skating, and thus she sacrificed little, but might gain much.

Accordingly after a rapid cup of coffee which was served in the long gallery, we left Madge comfortably reclined on the big sofa at right-angles to the fireplace, with an attractive book to beguile the tedium till tea. Being of the family, she knew all about handsome Dick and the babies, and the fate of Mrs. Canning and Colonel Blantyre, but as we went out I heard Blanche say to her, "Don't run it too fine, dear," and Madge had replied, "No, I'll go away well before sunset." And so we left her alone in the long gallery.

Madge read her attractive book for some minutes, but failing to get absorbed in it, put it down and limped across to the window. Though it was still but little after two, it was but a dim and uncertain light that entered, for the crystalline brightness of the morning had given place to a veiled obscurity produced by flocks of thick clouds which were coming sluggishly up from the northeast. Already the whole sky was overcast with them, and occasionally a few snowflakes fluttered waveringly down past the long windows. From the darkness and bitter cold of the afternoon, it seemed to her that there was like to be a heavy snowfall before long, and these outward signs were echoed inwardly in her by that muffled drowsiness of the brain, which to those who are sensitive to the pressures and lightness of weather portends storm. Madge was peculiarly the prey of such external influences: to her a brisk morning gave an ineffable brightness and briskness of spirit, and correspondingly the approach of heavy weather produced a somnolence in sensation that both drowsed and depressed her.

It was in such mood as this that she limped back again to the sofa beside the log-fire. The whole house was comfortably heated by water-pipes, and though the fire of logs and peat, an adorable mixture, had been allowed to burn low, the room was very warm. Idly she watched the dwindling flames, not opening her book again, but lying on the sofa with face towards the fireplace, intending drowsily and not immediately to go to her own room and spend the hours, until the return of the skaters made gaiety in the house again, in writing one or two neglected letters. Still drowsily she began thinking over what she had to communicate: one letter several days overdue should go to her mother, who was immensely interested in the psychical affairs of the family. She would tell her how Master Anthony had been prodigiously active on the staircase a night or two ago, and how the Blue Lady, regardless of the severity of the weather, had been seen by Mrs. Peveril that morning, strolling about. It was rather interesting: the Blue Lady had gone down the laurel walk and had been seen by her to enter the stables, where, at the moment, Freddy Peveril was inspecting the frost-bound hunters. Identically then, a sudden panic had spread through the stables, and the horses had whinnied and kicked, and shied, and sweated. Of the fatal twins nothing had been seen for many years past, but, as her mother knew, the Peverils never used the long gallery after dark.

Then for a moment she sat up, remembering that she was in the long gallery now. But it was still but a little after half-past two, and if she went to her room in half an hour, she would have ample time to write this and another letter before tea. Till then she would read her book. But she found she had left it on the window-sill, and it seemed scarcely worth while to get it. She felt exceedingly drowsy.

The sofa where she lay had been lately re-covered, in a greyish green shade of velvet, somewhat the color of lichen. It was of very thick, soft texture, and she luxuriously stretched her arms out, one on each side of her body, and pressed her fingers into the nap. How horrible that story of Mrs. Canning was: the growth on her face was of the color of lichen. And then without further transition or blurring of thought Madge fell asleep.

She dreamed. She dreamed that she awoke and found herself exactly where she had gone to sleep, and in exactly the same attitude. The flames from the logs had burned up again, and leaped on the walls, fitfully illuminating the picture of handsome Dick above the fireplace. In her dream she knew exactly what she had done today, and for what reason she was lying here now instead of being out with the rest of the skaters. She remembered also (still dreaming), that she was going to write a letter or two before tea, and prepared to get up in order to go to her room. As she half-rose she caught sight of her own arms lying out on each side of her on the grey velvet sofa. But she could not see where her hands ended, and where the grey velvet began: her fingers seemed to have melted into the stuff. She could see her wrists quite clearly, and a blue vein on the backs of her hands, and here and there a knuckle. Then, in her dream she remembered the last thought which had been in her mind before she fell asleep, namely the growth of the lichen-colored vegetation on the face and the eyes and the throat of Mrs. Canning. At that thought the strangling terror of real nightmare began: she knew that she was being transformed into this grey stuff, and she was absolutely unable to move. Soon the grey would spread up her arms, and over her feet; when they came in from skating they would find here nothing but a huge misshapen cushion of lichen-colored velvet, and that would be she. The horror grew more acute, and then by a violent effort she shook herself free of the clutches of this very evil dream, and she awoke.

For a minute or two she lay there, conscious only of the tremendous relief at finding herself awake. She felt again with her fingers the pleasant touch of the velvet, and drew them backwards and forwards, assuring herself that she was not, as her dream had suggested, melting into greyness and softness. But she was still, in spite of the violence of her awakening, very sleepy, and lay there till, looking down, she was aware that she could not see her hands at all. It was very nearly dark.

At that moment a sudden flicker of flame came from the dying fire, and a flare of burning gas from the peat flooded the room. The portrait of handsome Dick looked evilly down on her, and her hands were visible again. And then a panic worse than the panic of her dreams seized her. Daylight had altogether faded, and she knew that she was alone in the dark and terrible gallery. The panic was of the nature of nightmare, for she felt unable to move for terror. But it was worse than nightmare because she knew she was awake. And then the full cause of this frozen fear dawned on her; she knew with the certainty of absolute conviction that she was about to see the twin-babies.

She felt a sudden moisture break out on her face, and within her mouth her tongue and throat went suddenly dry, and she felt her tongue grate along the inner surface of her teeth. All power of movement had slipped from her limbs, leaving them dead and inert, and she stared with wide eyes into the blackness. The spurt of flame from the peat had burned itself out again, and darkness encompassed her.

Then on the wall opposite her, facing the windows, there grew a faint light of dusky crimson. For a moment she thought it but heralded the approach of the awful vision, then hope revived in her heart, and she remembered that thick clouds had overcast the sky before she went to sleep, and guessed that this light came from the sun not yet quite

sunk and set. This sudden revival of hope gave her the
necessary stimulus, and she sprang off the sofa where she lay.
She looked out of the window and saw the dull glow on the
horizon. But before she could take a step forward it was
obscured again. A tiny sparkle of light came from the hearth
which did not more than illuminate the tiles of the fireplace,
and snow falling heavily tapped at the window panes. There
was neither light nor sound except these.

But the courage that had come to her, giving her the power
of movement, had not quite deserted her, and she began
feeling her way down the gallery. And then she found that
she was lost. She stumbled against a chair, and, recovering
herself, stumbled against another. Then a table barred her
way, and, turning swiftly aside, she found herself up against
the back of the sofa. Once more she turned and saw the dim
gleam of the firelight on the side opposite to that on which
she expected it. In her blind gropings she must have reversed
her direction. But which way was she to go now? She seemed
blocked in by furniture. And all the time insistent and
imminent was the fact that the two innocent terrible ghosts
were about to appear to her.

Then she began to pray, "Lighten our darkness, O Lord,"
she said to herself. But she could not remember how the
prayer continued, and she had sore need of it. There was
something about the perils of the night. All this time she felt
about her with groping, fluttering hands. The fire-glimmer,
which should have been on her left, was on her right again;
therefore she must turn herself round again. "Lighten our
darkness," she whispered, and then aloud she repeated,
"Lighten our darkness."

She stumbled up against a screen, and could not remember
the existence of any such screen. Hastily she felt beside it
with blind hands, and touched something soft and velvety.
Was it the sofa on which she had lain? If so, where was the
head of it? It had a head and a back and feet—it was like a
person, all covered with grey lichen. Then she lost her head
completely. All that remained to her was to pray; she was
lost, lost in this awful place, where no one came in the dark

except the babies that cried. And she heard her voice rising from whisper to speech, and speech to scream. She shrieked out the holy words, she yelled them as if blaspheming as she groped among tables and chairs and the pleasant things of ordinary life which had become so terrible.

Then came a sudden and awful answer to her screamed prayer. Once more a pocket of inflammable gas in the peat on the hearth was reached by the smouldering embers, and the room started into light. She saw the evil eyes of handsome Dick, she saw the little ghostly snowflakes falling thickly outside. And she saw where she was, just opposite the door through which the terrible twins made their entrance. Then the flame went out again, and left her in blackness once more. But she had gained something, for she had her geography now. The center of the room was bare of furniture, and one swift dart would take her to the door of the landing above the main staircase and into safety. In that gleam she had been able to see the handle of the door, bright-brassed, luminous like a star. She would go straight for it; it was but a matter of a few seconds now.

She took a long breath, partly of relief, partly to satisfy the demands of her galloping heart. But the breath was only half-taken when she was stricken once more into the immobility of nightmare.

There came a little whisper, it was no more than that, from the door opposite which she stood, and through which the twin-babies entered. It was not quite dark outside, for she could see that the door was opening. And there stood in the opening two little white figures, side by side. They came towards her slowly, shufflingly. She could not see face or form at all distinctly, but the two little white figures were advancing. She knew them to be the ghosts of terror, innocent of the awful doom they were bound to bring, even as she was innocent. With the inconceivable rapidity of thought, she made up her mind what to do. She had not hurt them or laughed at them, and they, they were but babies when the wicked and bloody deed had sent them to their burning death. Surely the spirits of these children would not be inaccessible to the cry of one who was of the same blood as they, who had committed no fault that merited the doom they brought. If she entreated them they might have mercy, they might forbear to bring the curse upon her, they might allow her to pass out of the place without blight, without the sentence of death, or the shadow of things worse than death upon her.

It was but for the space of a moment that she hesitated, then she sank down on to her knees, and stretched out her hands towards them.

"Oh, my dears," she said, "I only fell asleep. I have done no more wrong than that—"

She paused a moment, and her tender girl's heart thought no more of herself, but only of them, those little innocent spirits on whom so awful a doom was laid, that they should bring death where other children bring laughter, and doom for delight. But all those who had seen them before had dreaded and feared them, or had mocked at them.

Then, as the enlightenment of pity dawned on her, her fear fell from her like the wrinkled sheath that holds the sweet folded buds of spring.

"Dears, I am so sorry for you," she said. "It is not your fault that you must bring me what you must bring, but I am not afraid any longer. I am only sorry for you. God bless you, you poor darlings."

She raised her head and looked at them. Though it was so dark, she could now see their faces, though all was dim and wavering, like the light of pale flames shaken by a draught. But the faces were not miserable or fierce—they smiled at her with shy little baby smiles. And as she looked they grew faint, fading slowly away like wreaths of vapor in frosty air.

Madge did not at once move when they had vanished, for instead of fear there was wrapped round her a wonderful sense of peace, so happy and serene that she would not willingly stir, and so perhaps disturb it. But before long she got up, and feeling her way, but without any sense of nightmare

pressing her on, or frenzy of fear to spur her, she went out of
the long gallery, to find Blanche just coming upstairs whis-
tling and swinging her skates.

"How's the leg, dear?" she asked. "You're not limping any
more."

Till that moment Madge had not thought of it.

"I think it must be all right," she said. "I had forgotten it
anyhow. Blanche, dear, you won't be frightened for me, will
you, but—I have seen the twins."

For a moment Blanche's face whitened with terror.

"What?" she said in a whisper.

"Yes, I saw them just now. But they were kind, they smiled
at me, and I was so sorry for them. And somehow I am sure I
have nothing to fear."

It seems that Madge was right, for nothing untoward has
come to her. Something, her attitude to them, we must suppose, her pity, her sympathy, touched and dissolved and
annihilated the curse. Indeed, I was at Church-Peveril only
last week, arriving there after dark. Just as I passed the
gallery door, Blanche came out.

"Ah, there you are," she said. "I've just been seeing the
twins. They looked too sweet and stopped nearly ten minutes. Let us have tea at once."

THE OLD NURSE'S STORY

Mrs. Gaskell

YOU KNOW, my dears, that your mother was an orphan, and an only child; and I dare say you have heard that your grandfather was a clergyman up in Westmorland, where I come from. I was just a girl in the village school, when, one day, your grandmother came in to ask the mistress if there was any scholar there who would do for a nurse maid; and mighty proud I was, I can tell ye, when the mistress called me up, and spoke to my being a good girl at my needle, and a steady, honest girl, and one whose parents were very respectable, though they might be poor. I thought I should like nothing better than to serve the pretty young lady, who was blushing as deep as I was as she spoke of the coming baby, and what I should have to do with it. However, I see you don't care so much for this part of my story as for what you think is to come, so I'll tell you at once. I was engaged and settled at the parsonage before Miss Rosamond (that was the baby, who is now your mother) was born. To be sure, I had little enough to do with her when she came, for she was never out of her mother's arms, and slept by her all night long; and proud enough was I sometimes when missis trusted her to me.

There never was such a baby before or since, though you've all of you been fine enough in your turns; but for sweet, winning ways, you've none of you come up to your mother. She took after her mother, who was a real lady born; a Miss Furnivall, a granddaughter of Lord Furnivall's, in North-

umberland. I believe she had neither brother nor sister, and
had been brought up in my lord's family till she had married
your grandfather, who was just a curate, son to a shopkeeper
in Carlisle—but a clever, fine gentleman as ever was—and one
who was a right-down hard worker in his parish, which was
very wide, and scattered all abroad over the Westmorland
Fells. When your mother, little Miss Rosamond, was about
four or five years old, both her parents died in a fortnight—
one after the other. Ah! that was a sad time. My pretty young
mistress and me was looking for another baby, when my
master came home from one of his long rides, wet and tired,
and took the fever he died of; and then she never held up her
head again, but just lived to see her dead baby, and have it
laid on her breast before she sighed away her life. My mistress
had asked me, on her death-bed, never to leave Miss Rosamond; but if she had never spoken a word, I would have gone
with the little child to the end of the world.

The next thing, and before we had well stilled our sobs,
the executors and guardians came to settle the affairs. They
were my poor young mistress's own cousin, Lord Furnivall,
and Mr. Esthwaithe, my master's brother, a shopkeeper in
Manchester; not so well-to-do then as he was afterwards, and
with a large family rising about him. Well! I don't know if it
were their settling, or because of a letter my mistress wrote
on her death-bed to her cousin, my lord; but somehow it was
settled that Miss Rosamond and me were to go to Furnivall
Manor House, in Northumberland, and my lord spoke as if it
had been her mother's wish that she should live with his
family, and as if he had no objections, for that one or two
more or less could make no difference in so grand a household. So though that was not the way in which I should have
wished the coming of my bright and pretty pet to have been
looked at—who was like a sunbeam to any family, be it ever
so grand—I was well pleased that all the folks in the Dale
should stare and admire when they heard I was going to be
young lady's maid at my Lord Furnivall's at Furnivall
Manor.

But I made a mistake in thinking we were to go and live

where my lord did. It turned out that the family had left Furnivall Manor House fifty years or more. I could not hear that my poor young mistress had ever been there, though she had been brought up in the family; and I was sorry for that, for I should have liked Miss Rosamond's youth to have passed where her mother's had been.

My lord's gentlemen, from whom I asked so many questions as I durst, said that the Manor House was at the foot of the Cumberland Fells, and a very grand place; that an old Miss Furnivall, a great-aunt of my lord's, lived there, with only a few servants; but that it was a very healthy place, and my lord had thought that it would suit Miss Rosamond very well for a few years, and that her being there might perhaps amuse his old aunt.

I was bidden by my lord to have Miss Rosamond's things ready by a certain day. He was a stern, proud man, as they say all the Lords Furnivall were; and he never spoke a word more than was necessary. Folk did say he had loved my young mistress; but that, because she knew that his father would object, she would never listen to him, and married Mr. Esthwaite, but I don't know. He never married, at any rate. But he never took much notice of Miss Rosamond; which I thought he might have done if he had cared for her dead mother. He sent his gentleman with us to Manor House, telling him to join him at Newcastle that same evening; so there was no great length of time for him to make us known to all the strangers before he, too, shook us off; and we were left, two lonely young things (I was not eighteen), in the great, old Manor House.

It seems like yesterday that we drove there. We had left our own dear parsonage very early, and we had both cried as if our hearts would break, though we were travelling in my lord's carriage, which I thought so much of once. And now it was long past noon on a September day, and we stopped to change horses for the last time at a little town all full of colliers and miners. Miss Rosamond had fallen asleep, but Mr. Henry told me to waken her, that she might see the park and the Manor House as we drove up. I thought it rather a pity; but I did what he bade me, for fear he should complain of me to my lord. We had left all signs of a town, or even a village, and were then inside the gates of a large wild park—not like the parks here in the north, but with rocks, and the noise of running water, and gnarled thorn-trees, and old oaks all white and peeled with age.

The road went up about two miles, and then we saw a great and stately house, with many trees close around it, so close that in some places their branches dragged against the walls when the wind blew; and some huge ones broken down; for no one seemed to take much charge of the place; to lop the wood, or to keep the moss-covered carriage-way in order. Only in front of the house all was clear. The great oval drive was without a weed; and neither tree nor creeper was allowed to grow over the long, many-windowed front; at both sides of which a wing projected, which were each the ends of other side fronts, for the house, although it was so desolate, was even grander than I expected. Behind it rose the Fells, which seemed unenclosed and bare enough; and on the left-hand of the house, as you stood facing it, was a little, old-fashioned flower garden, as I found out afterwards. A door opened out upon it from the west front; it had been scooped out of the thick dark wood for some old Lady Furnivall; but the branches of the great forest trees had grown and over-shadowed it again, and there were very few flowers that would live there at that time.

When we drove up to the great front entrance, and went into the hall I thought we should be lost—it was so large, and vast, and grand. There was a chandelier, all of bronze, hung down from the middle of the ceiling; and I had never seen one before, and looked at it all in amaze. Then, at one end of the hall, was a great fire-place, as large as the sides of the houses in my country, with massy andirons and dogs to hold the wood; and by it were heavy, old-fashioned sofas. At the opposite end of the hall, to the left as you went in—on the western side—was an organ built into the wall, and so large that it filled up the best part of that end. Beyond it, on the same side, was a door; and opposite, on each side of the fire-place, were also doors leading to the east front; but those I never went through as long as I stayed in the house, so I can't tell you what lay beyond.

The afternoon was closing in, and the hall, which had no fire lighted in it, looked dark and gloomy, but we did not stay there a moment. The old servant, who had opened the door for us, bowed to Mr. Henry, and took us in through the door at the farther side of the great organ, and led us through several smaller halls and passages into the west drawing-room, where he said that Miss Furnivall was sitting. Poor little Miss Rosamond held very tight to me, as if she were scared and lost in that great place, and as for myself, I was not much better. The west drawing-room was very cheerful-looking, with a warm fire in it, and plenty of wood, comfortable furni-ture about. Miss Furnivall was an old lady not far from eighty, I should think, but I do not know. She was thin and tall, and had a face as full of fine wrinkles as if they had been drawn all over it with a needle's point. Her eyes were very watchful, to make up, I suppose, for her being so deaf as to be obliged to use a trumpet.

Sitting with her, working at the same great piece of tapes-try, was Mrs. Stark, her maid and companion, and almost as old as she was. She had lived with Miss Furnivall ever since they were both young, and now she seemed more like a friend than a servant; she looked so cold and grey and stony— as if she had never loved or cared for anyone; and I don't suppose she did for anyone except her mistress; and, owing to the great deafness of the latter, Mrs. Stark treated her very much as if she were a child. Mr. Henry gave some message from my lord, and then he bowed good-bye to us all—taking no notice of my sweet little Miss Rosamond's outstretched hand—and left us standing there, being looked at by the two ladies through their spectacles.

I was right glad when they rung for the old footman who had shown us in at first, and told him to take us to our rooms. So we went out of that great drawing-room, and into another sitting-room, and out of that, and then up a great flight of stairs, and along a broad gallery—which was something like a library, having books all down one side and windows and writing-tables all down the other—till we came to our rooms, which I was not sorry to hear were just over the kitchens; for I began to think I should be lost in that wilderness of a house. There was an old nursery that had been used for all the little lords and ladies long ago, with a pleasant fire burning in the grate, and the kettle boiling on the hob, and tea-things spread out on the table; and out of that room was the night-nursery, with a little crib for Miss Rosamond close to my bed. And old James called up Dorothy, his wife, to bid us welcome; and both he and she were so hospitable and kind that by and by Miss Rosamond and me felt quite at home; and by the time tea was over, she was sitting on Dorothy's knee, and chattering away as fast as her little tongue could go.

I soon found out that Dorothy was from Westmorland, and that bound her and me together, as it were; and I would never wish to meet with kinder people than were old James and his wife. James had lived pretty nearly all his life in my lord's family, and thought there was no one so grand as they. He even looked down a little on his wife; because, till he had married her, she had never lived in any but a farmer's household. But he was very fond of her, as well he might be. They had one servant under them, to do all the rough work. Agnes, they called her; and she and me and James and Dorothy, with Miss Furnivall and Mrs. Stark, made up the family; always remembering my sweet Miss Rosamond. I used to wonder what they had done before she came, they thought so much of her now. Kitchen and drawing-room, it was all the same. The hard, sad Miss Furnivall, and the cold Mrs. Stark, looked pleased when she came fluttering in like a bird, playing and pranking hither and thither, with a continual murmur, and pretty prattle of gladness. I am sure they were sorry many a time when she flitted away into the kitchen, though they were too proud to ask her to stay with them, and were a little surprised at her taste; though to be sure, as Mrs. Stark said, it was not to be wondered at, remembering what stock her father had come of.

The great, old rambling house was a famous place for little Miss Rosamond. She made expeditions all over it, with me at her heels; all except the east wing, which was never opened, and whither we never thought of going. But in the western and northern part was many a pleasant room; full of things that were curiosities to us, though they might not have been to people who had seen more. The windows were darkened by the sweeping boughs of the trees, and the ivy which had overgrown them: but, in the green gloom, we could manage to see old China jars and carved ivory boxes, and great heavy books, and, above all, the old pictures.

Once, I remember, my darling would have Dorothy go with us to tell us who they all were; for they were all portraits of some of my lord's family, though Dorothy could not tell us the names of every one. We had gone through most of the rooms, when we came to the old state drawing-room over the hall, and there was a picture of Miss Furnivall; or, as she was called in those days, Miss Grace, for she was the younger sister. Such a beauty she must have been! but with such a set, proud look, and such scorn looking out of her handsome eyes, with her eyebrows just a little raised, as if she were wondering how anyone could have the impertinence to look at her; and her lip curled at us, as we stood there gazing. She had a dress on, the like of which I had never seen before, but it was all the fashion when she was young: a hat of some soft white stuff like beaver, pulled a little over her brows, and a beautiful plume of feathers sweeping round it on one side; and her gown of blue satin was open in front to a quilted white stomacher.

"Well, to be sure!" said I, when I had gazed my fill. "Flesh is grass, they do say; but who would have thought that Miss Furnivall had been such an out-and-out beauty, to see her now?"

"Yes," said Dorothy. "Folks change sadly. But if what my master's father used to say was true, Miss Furnivall, the elder sister, was handsomer than Miss Grace. Her picture is here

somewhere; but, if I show it you, you must never let on, even
to James, that you have seen it. Can the little lady hold her
tongue, think you?" asked she.

I was not so sure, for she was such a little sweet, bold, open-
spoken child, so I set her to hide herself; and then I helped
Dorothy to turn a great picture, that leaned with its face
towards the wall, and was not hung up as the others were. To
be sure, it beat Miss Grace for beauty; and, I think, for scorn-
ful pride too, though in that matter it might be hard to
choose. I could have looked at it an hour, but Dorothy
seemed half frightened at having shown it to me and hurried
it back again, and bade me run and find Miss Rosamond, for
that there were some ugly places about the house, where she
should like ill for the child to go. I was a brave, high-spirited
girl, and thought little of what the old woman said, for I
liked hide-and-seek as well as any child in the parish; so off I
ran to find my little one.

As winter drew on, and the days grew shorter, I was sometimes almost certain that I heard a noise as if someone was
playing on the great organ in the hall. I did not hear it every
evening; but, certainly, I did very often; usually when I was
sitting with Miss Rosamond, after I had put her to bed, and
keeping quite still and silent in the bedroom. Then I used to
hear it booming and swelling away in the distance. The first
night, when I went down to my supper, I asked Dorothy who
had been playing music, and James said very shortly that I
was a gowk to take the wind soughing among the trees for
music; but I saw Dorothy look at him very fearfully, and
Bessy, the kitchen-maid, said something beneath her breath,
and went quite white. I saw they did not like my question, so
I held my peace till I was with Dorothy alone, when I knew I
could get a good deal out of her.

So, the next day, I watched my time, and I coaxed and
asked her who it was that played the organ; for I knew that it
was the organ and not the wind well enough, for all I had
kept silence before James. But Dorothy had had her lesson,
I'll warrant, and never a word could I get from her. So then I
tried Bessy, though I had always held my head rather above

her, as I was evened to James and Dorothy, and she was little better than their servant. So she said I must never, never tell; and if I ever told, I was never to say *she* had told me; but it was a very strange noise, and she had heard it many a time, but most of all on winter nights, and before storms; and folks did say, it was the old lord playing on the great organ in the hall, just as he used to do when he was alive; but who the old lord was, or why he played, and why he played on stormy winter evenings in particular, she either could not or would not tell me. Well! I told you I had a brave heart; and I thought it was rather pleasant to have that grand music rolling about the house, let who would be the player; for now it rose above the great gusts of wind, and wailed and triumphed just like a living creature, and then it fell to a softness most complete; only it was always music and tunes, so it was nonsense to call it the wind.

I thought at first that it might be Miss Furnivall who played, unknown to Bessy; but one day when I was in the hall by myself, I opened the organ and peeped all above it and around it, as I had done to the organ in Crosthwaite Church once before, and I saw it was all broken and destroyed inside, though it looked so brave and fine; and then, though it was noonday, my flesh began to creep a little, and I shut it up, and ran away pretty quickly to my own bright nursery; and I did not like hearing the music for some time after that, any more than James and Dorothy did.

All this time Miss Rosamond was making herself more and more beloved. The old ladies liked her to dine with them at their early dinner; James stood behind Miss Furnivall's chair, and I behind Miss Rosamond's all in state; and, after dinner, she would play about in a corner of the great drawing-room, as still as any mouse, while Miss Furnivall slept, and I had my dinner in the kitchen. But she was glad enough to come to me in the nursery afterwards; for, as she said, Miss Furnivall was so sad, and Mrs. Stark so dull; but she and I were merry enough; and, by and by, I got not to care for that weird, rolling music, which did one no harm, if we did not know where it came from.

That winter was very cold. In the middle of October the frosts began, and lasted many, many weeks. I remember, one day at dinner, Miss Furnivall lifted up her sad, heavy eyes and said to Mrs. Stark, "I am afraid we shall have a terrible winter," in a strange kind of meaning way. But Mrs. Stark pretended not to hear, and talked very loud of something else. My little lady and I did not care for the frost; not we! As long as it was dry we climbed up the steep brows, behind the house, and went up on the Fells, which were bleak, and bare enough, and there we ran races in the fresh, sharp air; and once we came down by a new path that took us past the two old gnarled holly trees, which grew about half way down by the east side of the house.

But the days grew shorter and shorter; and the old lord—if it was he—played more and more stormily and sadly on the great organ. One Sunday afternoon—it must have been towards the end of November—I asked Dorothy to take charge of little Missy when she came out of the drawing-room, after Miss Furnivall had had her nap; for it was too cold to take her with me to church, and yet I wanted to go. And Dorothy was glad enough to promise, and was so fond of the child that all seemed well; and Bessy and I set off briskly, though the sky hung heavy and black over the white earth, as if the night had never fully gone away; and the air, though still, was very biting and keen.

"We shall have a fall of snow," said Bessy to me. And sure enough, even while we were in church, it came down thick, in great, large flakes, so thick it almost darkened the windows. It had stopped snowing before we came out, but it lay soft, thick, and deep beneath our feet as we tramped home. Before we got to the hall the moon rose, and I think it was lighter then—what with the moon, and what with the white dazzling snow—then it had been when we went to church, between two and three o'clock. I have not told you that Miss Furnivall and Mrs. Stark never went to church; they used to read the prayers together, in their quiet, gloomy way; they seemed to feel the Sunday very long with their tapestry-work to be busy at.

So when I went to Dorothy in the kitchen, to fetch Miss Rosamond and take her upstairs with me, I did not much wonder when the old woman told me that the ladies had kept the child with them, and that she had never come to the kitchen, as I had bidden her when she was tired of behaving pretty in the drawing-room. So I took off my things and went to find her, and bring her to her supper in the nursery. But when I went into the best drawing-room there sat the two old ladies, very still and quiet, dropping out a word now and then but looking as if nothing so bright and merry as Miss Rosamond had ever been near them. Still I thought she might be hiding from me; it was one of her pretty ways; and that she had persuaded them to look as if they knew nothing about her; so I went softly peeping under this sofa, and behind that chair, making believe I was sadly frightened at not finding her.

"What's the matter, Hester?" said Mrs. Stark sharply. I don't know if Miss Furnivall had seen me, for, as I told you, she was very deaf, and she sat quite still, idly staring into the fire, with her hopeless face. "I'm only looking for my little Rosy-Posy," I replied, still thinking that the child was there, and near me, though I could not see her.

"Miss Rosamond is not here," said Mrs. Stark. "She went away more than an hour ago to find Dorothy." And she too turned and went on looking into the fire.

My heart sank at this, and I began to wish I had never left my darling. I went back to Dorothy and told her. James was gone out for the day, but she and me and Bessy took lights and went up into the nursery first, and then we roamed over the great large house, calling and entreating Miss Rosamond to come out of her hiding-place, and not frighten us to death in that way. But there was no answer; no sound.

"Oh!" said I at last. "Can she have got into the east wing and hidden there?"

But Dorothy said it was not possible, for that she herself had never been there; that the doors were always locked, and my lord's steward had the keys, she believed; at any rate, neither she nor James had ever seen them. So I said I would go back and see if, after all, she was not hidden in the drawing-room, unknown to the old ladies; and if I found her there I said I would whip her well for the fright she had given me; but I never meant to do it. Well, I went back to the west drawing-room, and I told Mrs. Stark we could not find her anywhere, and asked for leave to look all about the furniture there, for I thought now, that she might have fallen asleep in some warm hidden corner; but no! we looked, Miss Furnivall got up and looked, trembling all over, and she was nowhere there; then we set off again, everyone in the house, and looked in all the places we had searched before, but we could not find her. Miss Furnivall shivered and shook so much that Mrs. Stark took her back into the warm drawing-room; but not before they had made me promise to bring her to them when she was found. Welladay! I began to think she never would be found, when I bethought me to look out into the great front court, all covered with snow.

I was upstairs when I looked out; but it was such clear moonlight I could see, quite plain, two little footprints, which might be traced from the hall door and round the corner of the east wing. I don't know how I got down, but I tugged open the great, stiff hall door; and, throwing the skirt of my own gown over my head for a cloak, I ran out. I turned the east corner, and there a black shadow fell on the snow; but when I came again into the moonlight, there were the little foot-marks going up—up to the Fells. It was bitter cold; so cold that the air almost took the skin off my face as I ran, but I ran on, crying to think how my poor little darling must be perished and frightened. I was within sight of the holly trees when I saw a shepherd coming down the hill, bearing something in his arms wrapped in his maud. He shouted to me, and asked me if I had lost a bairn; and, when I could not speak for crying, he bore towards me, and I saw my wee bairnie lying still, and white, and stiff in his arms, as if she had been dead. He told me he had been up the Fells to gather in his sheep, before the deep cold of night came on, and that under the holly trees (black marks on the hill-side, where no other bush was for miles around) he had found my little lady—my lamb—my queen—my darling—stiff and cold, in the terrible sleep which is frost-begotten.

Oh! the joy, and the tears of having her in my arms once again! for I would not let him carry her; but took her, maud and all, into my own arms, and held her near my own warm neck and heart, and felt the life stealing slowly back again into her little gentle limbs. But she was still insensible when we reached the hall, and I had no breath for speech. We went in by the kitchen door.

"Bring the warming-pan," said I; and I carried her upstairs, and began undressing her by the nursery fire, which Bessy had kept up. I called my little lammie all the sweet and playful names I could think of—even while my eyes were blinded by my tears; and at last, oh! at length she opened her large, blue eyes. Then I put her into her warm bed, and sent Dorothy down to tell Miss Furnivall that all was well; and I made up my mind to sit by my darling's bedside the live-long night. She fell away into a soft sleep as soon as her pretty head had touched the pillow, and I watched by her until morning light; when she wakened up bright and clear—or so I thought at first—and, my dears, so I think now.

She said that she had fancied that she should like to go to Dorothy, for that both the old ladies were asleep, and it was very dull in the drawing-room; and that, as she was going through the west lobby, she saw the snow through the high window falling—falling—soft and steady. But she wanted to see it lying pretty and white on the ground; so she made her way into the great hall; and then, going to the window, she saw it bright and soft upon the drive; but while she stood there, she saw a little girl, not so old as she was, "but so pretty," said my darling, "and this little girl beckoned to me to come out; and oh, she was so pretty and so sweet, I could not choose but go." And then this other little girl had taken her by the hand, and side by side the two had gone round the east corner.

"Now you are a naughty little girl, and telling stories,"

said I. "What would your good mamma, that is in heaven, and never told a story in her life, say to her little Rosamond, if she heard her—and I dare say she does—telling stories!"

"Indeed, Hester," sobbed out my child, "I'm telling you true. Indeed I am."

"Don't tell me!" said I, very stern. "I tracked you by your foot-marks through the snow; there were only yours to be seen; and if you had had a little girl to go hand in hand with you up the hill, don't you think the footprints would have gone along with yours?"

"I can't help it, dear, dear Hester," said she, crying, "if they did not. I never looked at her feet, but she held my hand fast and tight in her little one, and it was very, very cold. She took me up the Fell path, up to the holly trees; and there I saw a lady weeping and crying; but when she saw me, she hushed her weeping, and smiled very proud and grand, and took me on her knee, and began to lull me to sleep; and that's all, Hester—but that is true, and my dear mamma knows it is," said she, crying. So I thought the child was in a fever, and pretended to believe her, as she went over her story—over and over again, and always the same. At last Dorothy knocked at the door with Miss Rosamond's break-fast; and she told me the old ladies were down in the eating-parlour, and that they wanted to speak to me. They had both been into the night-nursery the evening before, but it was after Miss Rosamond was asleep; so they had only looked at her—not asked me any questions.

"I shall catch it," thought I to myself, as I went along the north gallery. "And yet," I thought, taking courage, "it was in their charge I left her; and it's they that's to blame for letting her steal away unknown and unwatched." So I went in boldly and told my story. I told it all to Miss Furnivall, shouting it close to her ear; but when I came to the mention of the other little girl out in the snow, coaxing and tempting her out, and willing her up to the grand and beautiful lady by the holly tree, she threw her arms up—her old and with-ered arms—and cried aloud, "Oh! Heaven, forgive! Have mercy!"

Mrs. Stark took hold of her; roughly enough, I thought; but she was past Mrs. Stark's management, and spoke to me, in a kind of wild warning and authority.

"Hester, keep her from that child! It will lure her to her death! That evil child! Tell her it is a wicked, naughty child." Then Mrs. Stark hurried me out of the room; where, indeed, I was glad enough to go; but Miss Furnivall kept shrieking out, "Oh! have mercy! Wilt Thou never forgive! It is many a long year ago—"

I was very uneasy in my mind after that. I durst never leave Miss Rosamond, night or day, for fear lest she might slip off again, after some fancy or other; and all the more because I thought I could make out that Miss Furnivall was crazy, from their odd ways about her; and I was afraid lest something of the same kind (which might be in the family, you know) hung over my darling. And the great frost never ceased all this time; and whenever it was a more stormy night than usual, between the gusts, and through the wind, we heard the old lord playing on the great organ. But, old lord or not, wherever Miss Rosamond went, there I followed; for my love for her, pretty, helpless orphan, was stronger than fear for the grand and terrible sound. Besides, it rested with me to keep her cheerful and merry, as beseemed her age. So we played together, and wandered together, here and there, and everywhere; for I never dared to lose sight of her again in that large and rambling house. And so it happened, that one afternoon, not long before Christmas Day, we were playing together on the billiard-table in the great hall (not that we knew the way of playing, but she liked to roll the smooth, ivory balls with her pretty hands, and I liked to do whatever she did); and, by and by, without our noticing it, it grew dusk indoors, though it was still light in the open air, and I was thinking of taking her back into the nursery, when, all of a sudden, she cried out:

"Look! Hester, look! there is my poor little girl out in the snow!"

I turned towards the long narrow windows, and there, sure enough, I saw a little girl, less than my Miss Rosamond—

dressed all unfit to be out of doors such a bitter night—crying, and beating against the window-panes, as if she wanted to be let in. She seemed to sob and wail, till Miss Rosamond could bear it no longer, and was flying to the door to open it, when, all of a sudden, and close up upon us, the great organ pealed out so loud and thundering, it fairly made me tremble; and all the more, when I remembered me that, even in the stillness of that dead-cold weather, I had heard no sound of little battering hands upon the window glass, although the Phantom Child had seemed to put forth all its force; and, although I had seen it wail and cry, no faintest touch of sound had fallen upon my ears. Whether I remembered all this at the very moment, I do not know; the great organ sound had so stunned me into terror; but this I know: I caught up Miss Rosamond before she got the hall door opened, and clutched her, and carried her away, kicking and screaming, into the large bright kitchen, where Dorothy and Agnes were busy with their mince pies.

"What is the matter with my sweet one?" cried Dorothy, as I bore in Miss Rosamond, who was sobbing as if her heart would break.

"She won't let me open the door for my little girl to come in; and she'll die if she is out on the Fells all night. Cruel, naughty Hester," she said, slapping me; but she might have struck harder, for I had seen a look of ghastly terror on Dorothy's face, which made my very blood run cold.

"Shut the back-kitchen door fast, and bolt it well," said she to Agnes. She said no more; she gave me raisins and almonds to quiet Miss Rosamond: but she sobbed about the little girl in the snow, and would not touch any of the good things. I was thankful when she cried herself to sleep in bed. Then I stole down to the kitchen and told Dorothy I had made up my mind. I would carry my darling back to my father's house in Applethwaite; where, if we lived humbly, we lived at peace. I said I had been frightened enough with the old lord's organ-playing; but now that I had seen for myself this little moaning child, all decked out as no child in the neighbourhood could be, beating and battering to get in, yet always without any sound or noise—with the dark wound on her right shoulder; and that Miss Rosamond had known it again for the phantom that had nearly lured her to her death (which Dorothy knew was true) ; I would stand it no longer.

I saw Dorothy change colour once or twice. When I had done she told me she did not think I could take Miss Rosamond with me, for that she was my lord's ward, and I had no right over her; and she asked me, would I leave the child that I was so fond of just for sounds and sights that could do me no harm; and that they had all had to get used to in their turns? I was all in a hot, trembling passion; and I said it was very well for her to talk, that knew what these sights and noises betokened, and that had, perhaps, had something to do with the Spectre Child while it was alive. And I taunted her so, that she told me all she knew, at last, and then I wished I had never been told, for it only made me afraid more than ever.

She said she had heard the tale from old neighbours, that were alive when she was first married; when folks used to come to the hall sometimes, before it had got such a bad name on the country-side: it might not be true, or it might, what she had been told.

The old lord was Miss Furnivall's father—Miss Grace, as Dorothy called her, for Miss Maude was the elder, and Miss Furnivall by rights. The old lord was eaten up with pride. Such a proud man was never seen or heard of; and his daughters were like him. No one was good enough to wed them, although they had choice enough; for they were the great beauties of their day, as I had seen by their portraits where they hung in the state drawing-room. But, as the old saying is, "Pride will have a fall"; and these two haughty beauties fell in love with the same man, and he no better than a foreign musician whom their father had down from London to play music with him at the Manor House. For above all things, next to his pride, the old lord loved music. He could play on nearly every instrument that ever was heard of: and it was a strange thing it did not soften him; but he was a fierce, dour old man, and had broken his poor wife's heart with his cruelty, they said. He was mad after music, and would pay any money for it. So he got this foreigner to come; who made such beautiful music, that they said the very birds on the trees stopped their singing to listen. And, by degrees, this foreign gentleman got such a hold over the old lord that nothing would serve him but that he must come every year; and it was he that had the great organ brought from Holland and built up in the hall, where it stood now. He taught the old lord to play on it; but many and many a time, when Lord Furnivall was thinking of nothing but his fine organ, and his finer music, the dark foreigner was walking abroad in the woods with one of the young ladies; now Miss Maude, and then Miss Grace.

Miss Maude won the day and carried off the prize—such as it was; and he and she were married, all unknown to anyone; and before he made his next yearly visit, she had been confined of a little girl at a farm-house on the Moors, while her father and Miss Grace thought she was away at Doncaster Races. But though she was a wife and a mother she was not a bit softened, but as haughty and as passionate as ever; and perhaps more so, for she was jealous of Miss Grace, to whom her foreign husband paid a deal of court—by way of blinding her—as he told his wife. But Miss Grace triumphed over Miss Maude, and Miss Maude grew fiercer and fiercer, both with her husband and with her sister; and the former—who could easily shake off what was disagreeable, and hide himself in foreign countries—went away a month before his usual time that summer, and half threatened that he would never come back again.

Meanwhile, the little girl was left at the farm-house, and her mother used to have her horse saddled and gallop wildly over the hills to see her once every week at the very least—for where she loved, she loved; and where she hated, she hated. And the old lord went on playing—playing on his organ; and the servants thought the sweet music he made had soothed down his awful temper, of which (Dorothy said) some terrible tales could be told. He grew infirm too, and had to walk with a crutch; and his son—that was the present Lord Furnivall's father—was with the army in America, and the other son at sea; so Miss Maude had it pretty much her own way, and she and Miss Grace grew colder and bitterer to each other every day; till at last they hardly ever spoke, except when the old lord was by. The foreign musician came again the next summer, but it was for the last time; for they led him such a life with their jealousy and their passions that he grew weary, and went away, and never was heard of again. And Miss Maude, who had always meant to have her marriage acknowledged when her father should be dead, was left now a deserted wife—whom nobody knew to have been married—with a child that she dared not own, although she loved it to distraction; living with a father whom she feared, and a sister whom she hated.

When the next summer passed over and the dark foreigner never came, both Miss Maude and Miss Grace grew gloomy and sad; they had a haggard look about them, though they looked handsome as ever. But by and by Miss Maude brightened; for her father grew more and more infirm, and more than ever carried away by his music; and she and Miss Grace lived almost entirely apart, having separate rooms, the one on the west side, Miss Maude on the east—those very rooms which were now shut up. So she thought she might have her little girl with her, and no one need ever know except those who dared not speak about it, and were bound to believe that it was, as she said, a cottager's child she had taken a fancy to. All this, Dorothy said, was pretty well known; but what came afterwards no one knew, except Miss Grace and Mrs. Stark, who was even then her maid, and much more of a friend to her than ever her sister had been. But the servants supposed, from words that were dropped, that Miss Maude had triumphed over Miss Grace, and told her that all the time the dark foreigner had been mocking her with pretended love he was her own husband; the colour left Miss Grace's cheek and lips that very day for ever, and she was heard to say many a time that sooner or later she would have her revenge; and Mrs. Stark was for ever spying about the east rooms.

One fearful night, just after the New Year had come in,

when the snow was lying thick and deep, and the flakes were still falling—fast enough to blind any one who might be out and abroad—there was a great and violent noise heard, and the old lord's voice above all, cursing and swearing awfully; and the cries of a little child; and the proud defiance of a fierce woman; and the sound of a blow; and a dead stillness; and moans and wailings dying away on the hill-side! Then the old lord summoned all his servants, and told them, with terrible oaths, and words more terrible, that his daughter had disgraced herself, and that he had turned her out of doors— her, and her child—and that if ever they gave her help, or food, or shelter, he prayed that they might never enter heaven. And, all the while, Miss Grace stood by him, white and still as any stone; and when he had ended she heaved a great sigh, as much as to say her work was done, and her end was accomplished. But the old lord never touched his organ again, and died within the year; and no wonder! for, on the morrow of that wild and fearful night, the shepherds coming down the Fell side, found Miss Maude sitting all crazy and smiling, under the holly trees, nursing a dead child—with a terrible mark on its right shoulder. "But that was not what killed it," said Dorothy; "it was the frost and the cold. Every wild creature was in its hole, and every beast in its fold— while the child and its mother were turned out to wander on the Fells! And now you know all, and I wonder if you are less frightened now?"

I was more frightened than ever; but I said I was not. I wished Miss Rosamond and myself well out of that dreadful house for ever; but I would not leave her, and I dared not take her away. But oh! how I watched her, and guarded her! We bolted the doors and shut the window-shutters fast, and an hour or more before dark rather than leave them open five minutes too late. But my little lady still heard the weird child crying and mourning; and not all we could do or say could keep her from wanting to go to her, and let her in from the cruel wind and the snow. All this time, I kept away from Miss Furnivall and Mrs. Stark as much as ever I could; for I feared them—I knew no good could be about them, with their grey, hard faces, and their dreamy eyes looking back into the ghastly years that were gone. But, even in my fear, I had a kind of pity—for Miss Furnivall, at least. Those gone down to the pit can hardly have a more hopeless look than that which was ever on her face. At last I even got so sorry for her—who never said a word but what was quite forced from her—that I prayed for her; and I taught Miss Rosamond to pray for one who had done a deadly sin; but often, when she came to those words, she would listen, and start up from her knees, and say, "I hear my little girl plaining and crying very sad—Oh! let her in, or she will die!"

One night—just after New Year's Day had come at last, and the long winter had taken a turn, as I hoped—I heard the west drawing-room bell ring three times, which was a signal for me. I would not leave Miss Rosamond alone, for all she was asleep—for the old lord had been playing wilder than ever—and I feared lest my darling should waken to hear the Spectre Child; see her I knew she could not—I had fastened the windows too well for that. So I took her out of her bed and wrapped her up in such outer clothes as were most handy, and carried her down to the drawing-room, where the old ladies sat at their tapestry-work as usual. They looked up when I came in, and Mrs. Stark asked, quite astounded, "Why did I bring Miss Rosamond there, out of her warm bed?" I had begun to whisper, "Because I was afraid of her being tempted out while I was away, by the wild child in the snow," when she stopped me short (with a glance at Miss Furnivall), and said Miss Furnivall wanted me to undo some work she had done wrong, and which neither of them could see to unpick. So I laid my pretty dear on the sofa, and sat down on a stool by them, and hardened my heart against them, as I heard the wind rising and howling.

Miss Rosamond slept on sound, for all the wind blew so; and Miss Furnivall said never a word, nor looked round when the gusts shook the windows. All at once she started up to her full height, and put up one hand, as if to bid us listen.

"I hear voices!" said she, "I hear terrible screams—I hear my father's voice!"

Just at that moment my darling wakened with a sudden start: "My little girl is crying, oh, how she is crying!" and she tried to get up and go to her, but she got her feet entangled in the blanket, and I caught her up; for my flesh had begun to creep at these noises, which they heard while we could catch no sound. In a minute or two the noises came, gathered fast, and filled our ears; we, too, heard voices and screams, and no longer heard the winter's wind that raged abroad. Mrs. Stark looked at me, and I at her, but we dared not speak. Suddenly Miss Furnivall went towards the door, out into the ante-room, through the west lobby, and opened the door into the great hall. Mrs. Stark followed, and I durst not be left, though my heart almost stopped beating for fear. I wrapped my darling tight in my arms and went out with them. In the hall the screams were louder than ever; they sounded to come from the east wing—nearer and nearer—close on the other side of the locked-up doors—close behind them. Then I noticed that the great bronze chandelier seemed all alight, though the hall was dim, and that a fire was blazing in the vast hearth-place, though it gave no heat; and I shuddered up with terror, and folded my darling closer to me. But as I did so, the east door shook, and she, suddenly struggling to get free from me, cried, "Hester, I must go! My little girl is there; I hear her; she is coming! Hester, I must go!"

I held her tight with all my strength; with a set will, I held her. If I had died my hands would have grasped her still, I was so resolved in my mind. Miss Furnivall stood listening, and paid no regard to my darling, who had got down to the ground and whom I, upon my knees now, was holding with both my arms clasped round her neck; she still striving and crying to get free.

All at once the east door gave way with a thundering crash, as if torn open in a violent passion, and there came into that broad and mysterious light the figure of a tall old man, with grey hair and gleaming eyes. He drove before him, with many a relentless gesture of abhorrence, a stern and beautiful woman, with a little child clinging to her dress.

"Oh, Hester! Hester! cried Miss Rosamond. "It's the lady! the lady below the holly trees; and my little girl is with her. Hester! Hester! let me go to her; they are drawing me to them. I feel them, I feel them. I must go!"

Again she was almost convulsed by her efforts to get away; but I held her tighter and tighter, till I feared I should do her a hurt; but rather that than let her go towards those terrible phantoms. They passed along towards the great hall door, where the winds howled and ravened for their prey; but before they reached that, the lady turned; and I could see that she defied the old man with a fierce and proud defiance; but then she quailed—and then she threw up her arms wildly and piteously to save her child—her little child—from a blow from his uplifted crutch.

And Miss Rosamond was torn as by a power stronger than mine, and writhed in my arms, and sobbed (for by this time the poor darling was growing faint) .

"They want me to go with them on to the Fells—they are drawing me to them. Oh, my little girl! I would come, but cruel, wicked Hester holds me very tight." But when she saw the uplifted crutch she swooned away, and I thanked God for it. Just at this moment—when the tall old man, his hair streaming as in the blast of a furnace, was going to strike the little shrinking child—Miss Furnivall, the old woman by my side cried out, "Oh, Father! Father! spare the little innocent child!" But just then I saw—we all saw—another phantom shape itself, and grow clear out of the blue and misty light that filled the hall; we had not seen her till now, for it was another lady who stood by the old man, with a look of relentless hate and triumphant scorn. That figure was very beautiful to look upon, with a soft white hat drawn down over the proud brows and a red and curling lip. It was dressed in an open robe of blue satin. I had seen that figure before. It was the likeness of Miss Furnivall in her youth; and the terrible phantoms moved on, regardless of old Miss Furnivall's wild entreaty—and the uplifted crutch fell on the right shoulder of the little child, and the younger sister looked on, stony and deadly serene. But at that moment the dim lights and the fire

that gave no heat went out of themselves, and Miss Furnivall
lay at our feet stricken down by the palsy—death stricken.

Yes, she was carried to her bed that night never to rise
again. She lay with her face to the wall muttering low but
muttering always: "Alas! alas! what is done in youth can
never be undone in age! What is done in youth can never be
undone in age!"

LOST HEARTS

M. R. James

IT WAS, as far as I can ascertain, in September of the year 1811 that a post-chaise drew up before the door of Aswarby Hall, in the heart of Lincolnshire. The little boy who was the only passenger in the chaise, and who jumped out as soon as it had stopped, looked about him with the keenest curiosity during the short interval that elapsed between the ringing of the bell and the opening of the hall door. He saw a tall, square, red-brick house, built in the reign of Anne; a stone-pillared porch had been added in the purer classical style of 1790; the windows of the house were many, tall and narrow, with small panes and thick white woodwork. A pediment, pierced with a round window, crowned the front. There were wings to right and left, connected by curious glazed galleries, supported by colonnades, with the central block. These wings plainly contained the stables and offices of the house. Each was surmounted by an ornamental cupola with a gilded vane.

An evening light shone on the building, making the window-panes glow like so many fires. Away from the Hall in front stretched a flat park studded with oaks and fringed with firs, which stood out against the sky. The clock in the church-tower, buried in trees on the edge of the park, only its golden weathercock catching the light, was striking six, and the sound came gently beating down the wind. It was altogether a pleasant impression, though tinged with the sort of melancholy appropriate to an evening in early autumn, that was conveyed to the mind of the boy who was standing in the porch waiting for the door to open to him.

The post-chaise had brought him from Warwickshire, where, some six months before, he had been left an orphan. Now, owing to the generous offer of his elderly cousin, Mr. Abney, he had come to live at Aswarby. The offer was unexpected, because all who knew anything of Mr. Abney looked upon him as a somewhat austere recluse, into whose steady-going household the advent of a small boy would import a new and, it seemed, incongruous element. The truth is that very little was known of Mr. Abney's pursuits or temper. The Professor of Greek at Cambridge had been heard to say that no one knew more of the religious beliefs of the later pagans than did the owner of Aswarby. Certainly his library contained all the then available books bearing on the Mysteries, the Orphic poems, the worship of Mithras, and the Neo-Platonists. In the marble-paved hall stood a fine group of Mithras slaying a bull, which had been imported from the Levant at great expense by the owner. He had contributed a description of it to the *Gentleman's Magazine,* and he had written a remarkable series of articles in the *Critical Museum* on the superstitions of the Romans of the Lower Empire. He was looked upon, in fine, as a man wrapped up in his books, and it was a matter of great surprise among his neighbours that he should even have heard of his orphan cousin, Stephen Elliott, much more that he should have volunteered to make him an inmate of Aswarby Hall.

Whatever may have been expected by his neighbours, it is certain that Mr. Abney—the tall, the thin, the austere—seemed inclined to give his young cousin a kindly reception. The moment the front door was opened he darted out of his study, rubbing his hands with delight.

"How are you, my boy?—how are you? How old are you?" said he— "that is, you are not too much tired, I hope, by your journey to eat your supper?"

"No, thank you, sir," said Master Elliott; "I am pretty well."

"That's a good lad," said Mr. Abney. "And how old are you, my boy?"

It seemed a little odd that he should have asked the question twice in the first two minutes of their acquaintance.

"I'm twelve years old next birthday, sir," said Stephen.

"And when is your birthday, my dear boy? Eleventh of September, eh? That's well—that's very well. Nearly a year hence, isn't it? I like—ha, ha!—I like to get these things down in my book. Sure it's twelve? Certain?"

"Yes, quite sure, sir."

"Well, well! Take him to Mrs. Bunch's room, Parkes, and let him have his tea—supper—whatever it is."

"Yes, sir," answered the staid Mr. Parkes; and conducted Stephen to the lower regions.

Mrs. Bunch was the most comfortable and human person whom Stephen had as yet met in Aswarby. She made him completely at home; they were great friends in a quarter of an hour: and great friends they remained. Mrs. Bunch had been born in the neighbourhood some fifty-five years before the date of Stephen's arrival, and her residence at the Hall was of twenty years' standing. Consequently, if anyone knew the ins and outs of the house and the district, Mrs. Bunch knew them; and she was by no means disinclined to communicate her information.

Certainly there were plenty of things about the Hall and the Hall gardens which Stephen, who was of an adventurous and inquiring turn, was anxious to have explained to him. "Who built the temple at the end of the laurel walk? Who was the old man whose picture hung on the staircase, sitting at a table, with a skull under his hand?" These and many similar points were cleared up by the resources of Mrs. Bunch's powerful intellect. There were others, however, of which the explanations furnished were less satisfactory.

One November evening Stephen was sitting by the fire in the housekeeper's room reflecting on his surroundings.

"Is Mr. Abney a good man, and will he go to heaven?" he suddenly asked, with the peculiar confidence which children possess in the ability of their elders to settle these questions, the decision of which is believed to be reserved for other tribunals.

"Good?—bless the child!" said Mrs. Bunch. "Master's as kind a soul as ever I see! Didn't I never tell you of the little boy as he took in out of the street, as you may say, this seven years back? and the little girl, two years after I first come here?"

"No. Do tell me all about them, Mrs. Bunch—now this minute!"

"Well," said Mrs. Bunch, "the little girl I don't seem to recollect so much about. I know master brought her back with him from his walk one day, and give orders to Mrs. Ellis, as was housekeeper then, as she should be took every care with. And the poor child hadn't no one belonging to her—she told me so her own self—and here she lived with us a matter of three weeks it might be; and then, whether she were some-think of a gipsy in her blood or what not, but one morning she out of her bed afore any of us had opened a eye, and neither track nor yet trace of her have I set eyes on since. Master was wonderful put about, and had all the ponds dragged; but it's my belief she was had away by them gipsies, for there was singing round the house for as much as an hour the night she went, and Parkes, he declare as he heard them a-calling in the woods all that afternoon. Dear, dear! a hodd child she was, so silent in her ways and all, but I was wonder-ful taken up with her, so domesticated she was—surprising."

"And what about the little boy?" said Stephen.

"Ah, that poor boy!" sighed Mrs. Bunch. "He were a foreigner—Jevanny he called hisself—and he come a-tweaking his 'urdy-gurdy round and about the drive one winter day, and master 'ad him in that minute, and ast all about where he came from, and how old he was, and how he made his way, and where was his relatives, and all as kind as heart could wish. But it went the same way with him. They're a hunruly lot, them foreign nations, I do suppose, and he was off one fine morning just the same as the girl. Why he went and what he done was our question for as much as a year after; for he never took his 'urdy-gurdy, and there it lays on the shelf."

The remainder of the evening was spent by Stephen in miscellaneous cross-examination of Mrs. Bunch and in efforts to extract a tune from the hurdy-gurdy.

That night he had a curious dream. At the end of the passage at the top of the house, in which his bedroom was situated, there was an old disused bathroom. It was kept locked, but the upper half of the door was glazed, and, since the muslin curtains which used to hang there had long been gone, you could look in and see the lead-lined bath affixed to the wall on the right hand, with its head towards the window.

On the night of which I am speaking, Stephen Elliott found himself, as he thought, looking through the glazed door. The moon was shining through the window, and he was gazing at a figure which lay in the bath.

His description of what he saw reminds me of what I once beheld myself in the famous vaults of St. Michan's Church in Dublin, which possess the horrid property of preserving corpses from decay for centuries. A figure inexpressibly thin and pathetic, of a dusty leaden colour, enveloped in a shroud-like garment, the thin lips crooked into a faint and dreadful smile, the hands pressed tightly over the region of the heart.

As he looked upon it, a distant, almost inaudible moan seemed to issue from its lips, and the arms began to stir. The terror of the sight forced Stephen backwards, and he awoke to the fact that he was indeed standing on the cold boarded floor of the passage in the full light of the moon. With a courage which I do not think can be common among boys of his age, he went to the door of the bathroom to ascertain if the figure of his dream were really there. It was not, and he went back to bed.

Mrs. Bunch was much impressed next morning by his story, and went so far as to replace the muslin curtain over the glazed door of the bathroom. Mr. Abney, moreover, to whom he confided his experiences at breakfast, was greatly interested, and made notes of the matter in what he called "his book."

The spring equinox was approaching, as Mr. Abney frequently reminded his cousin, adding that this had been always considered by the ancients to be a critical time for the young: that Stephen would do well to take care of himself, and to shut his bedroom window at night; and that Censorinus had some valuable remarks on the subject. Two incidents that occurred about this time made an impression upon Stephen's mind.

The first was after an unusually uneasy and oppressed night that he had passed—though he could not recall any particular dream that he had had.

The following evening Mrs. Bunch was occupying herself in mending his nightgown.

"Gracious me, Master Stephen!" she broke forth rather irritably, "how do you manage to tear your nightdress all to flinders this way? Look here, sir, what trouble you do give to poor servants that have to darn and mend after you!"

There was indeed a most destructive and apparently wanton series of slits or scorings in the garment, which would undoubtedly require a skilful needle to make good. They were confined to the left side of the chest—long, parallel slits, about six inches in length, some of them not quite piercing the texture of the linen. Stephen could only express his entire ignorance of their origin: he was sure they were not there the night before.

"But," he said, "Mrs. Bunch, they are just the same as the scratches on the outside of my bedroom door; and I'm sure I never had anything to do with making *them*."

Mrs. Bunch gazed at him open-mouthed, then snatched up a candle, departed hastily from the room, and was heard making her way upstairs. In a few minutes she came down.

"Well," she said, "Master Stephen, it's a funny thing to me how them marks and scratches can 'a' come there—too high up for any cat or dog to 'ave made 'em, much less a rat: for all the world like a Chinaman's finger-nails, as my uncle in the tea-trade used to tell us of when we was girls together. I wouldn't say nothing to master, not if I was you, Master Stephen, my dear; and just turn the key of the door when you go to your bed."

"I always do, Mrs. Bunch, as soon as I've said my prayers."

"Ah, that's a good child: always say your prayers, and then no one can't hurt you."

Herewith Mrs. Bunch addressed herself to mending the injured nightgown, with intervals of meditation, until bedtime. This was on a Friday night in March, 1812.

On the following evening the usual duet of Stephen and Mrs. Bunch was augmented by the sudden arrival of Mr. Parkes, the butler, who as a rule kept himself rather *to* himself in his own pantry. He did not see that Stephen was there: he was, moreover, flustered, and less slow of speech than was his wont.

"Master may get up his own wine, if he likes, of an evening," was his first remark. "Either I do it in the daytime or not at all, Mrs. Bunch. I don't know what it may be: very like it's the rats, or the wind got into the cellars; but I'm not so young as I was, and I can't go through with it as I have done."

"Well, Mr. Parkes, you know it is a surprising place for the rats, is the Hall."

"I'm not denying that, Mrs. Bunch; and, to be sure, many a time I've heard the tale from the men in the shipyards about the rat that could speak. I never laid no confidence in that before; but to-night, if I'd demeaned myself to lay my ear to the door of the further bin, I could pretty much have heard what they was saying."

"Oh, there, Mr. Parkes, I've no patience with your fancies! Rats talking in the wine-cellar indeed!"

"Well, Mrs. Bunch, I've no wish to argue with you: all I say is, if you choose to go to the far bin, and lay your ear to the door, you may prove my words this minute."

"What nonsense you do talk, Mr. Parkes—not fit for children to listen to! Why, you'll be frightening Master Stephen there out of his wits."

"What! Master Stephen?" said Parkes, awaking to the consciousness of the boy's presence. "Master Stephen knows well enough when I'm a-playing a joke with you, Mrs. Bunch."

In fact, Master Stephen knew much too well to suppose

that Mr. Parkes had in the first instance intended a joke. He
was interested, not altogether pleasantly, in the situation; but
all his questions were unsuccessful in inducing the butler to
give any more detailed account of his experiences in the wine-
cellar.

We have now arrived at March 24, 1812. It was a day of
curious experiences for Stephen: a windy, noisy day, which
filled the house and the gardens with a restless impression. As
Stephen stood by the fence of the grounds, and looked out
into the park, he felt as if an endless procession of unseen
people were sweeping past him on the wind, borne on resist-
lessly and aimlessly, vainly striving to stop themselves, to
catch at something that might arrest their flight and bring
them once again into contact with the living world of which
they had formed a part. After luncheon that day Mr. Abney
said:

"Stephen, my boy, do you think you could manage to come
to me to-night as late as eleven o'clock in my study? I shall be
busy until that time, and I wish to show you something
connected with your future life which it is most important
that you should know. You are not to mention this matter to
Mrs. Bunch nor to anyone else in the house; and you had
better go to your room at the usual time."

Here was a new excitement added to life: Stephen eagerly
grasped at the opportunity of sitting up till eleven o'clock.
He looked in at the library door on his way upstairs that
evening, and saw a brazier, which he had often noticed in the
corner of the room, moved out before the fire; an old silver-
gilt cup stood on the table, filled with red wine, and some
written sheets of paper lay near it. Mr. Abney was sprinkling
some incense on the brazier from a round silver box as
Stephen passed, but did not seem to notice his step.

The wind had fallen, and there was a still night and a full
moon. At about ten o'clock Stephen was standing at the open
window of his bedroom, looking out over the country. Still as
the night was, the mysterious population of the distant
moonlit woods was not yet lulled to rest. From time to time

strange cries as of lost and despairing wanderers sounded
from across the mere. They might be the notes of owls or
water-birds, yet they did not quite resemble either sound.
Were not they coming nearer? Now they sounded from the
nearer side of the water, and in a few moments they seemed
to be floating about among the shrubberies. Then they
ceased; but just as Stephen was thinking of shutting the
window and resuming his reading of *Robinson Crusoe*, he
caught sight of two figures standing on the gravelled terrace
that ran along the garden side of the Hall—the figures of a
boy and girl, as it seemed; they stood side by side, looking up
at the windows. Something in the form of the girl recalled
irresistibly his dream of the figure in the bath. The boy
inspired him with more acute fear.

Whilst the girl stood still, half smiling, with her hands
clasped over her heart, the boy, a thin shape, with black hair
and ragged clothing, raised his arms in the air with an appearance of menace and of unappeasable hunger and longing. The moon shone upon his almost transparent hands, and
Stephen saw that the nails were fearfully long and that the
light shone through them. As he stood with his arms thus
raised, he disclosed a terrifying spectacle. On the left side of
his chest there opened a black and gaping rent; and there fell
upon Stephen's brain, rather than upon his ear, the impression of one of those hungry and desolate cries that he had
heard resounding over the woods of Aswarby all that evening. In another moment this dreadful pair had moved
swiftly and noiselessly over the dry gravel, and he saw them
no more.

Inexpressibly frightened as he was, he determined to take
his candle and go down to Mr. Abney's study, for the hour
appointed for their meeting was near at hand. The study or
library opened out of the front hall on one side, and Stephen,
urged on by his terrors, did not take long in getting there. To
effect an entrance was not so easy. The door was not locked,
he felt sure, for the key was on the outside of it as usual. His
repeated knocks produced no answer. Mr. Abney was engaged: he was speaking. What! why did he try to cry out? and

why was the cry choked in his throat? Had he, too, seen the mysterious children? But now everything was quiet, and the door yielded to Stephen's terrified and frantic pushing.

On the table in Mr. Abney's study certain papers were found which explained the situation to Stephen Elliott when he was of an age to understand them. The most important sentences were as follows:

"It was a belief very strongly and generally held by the ancients—of whose wisdom in these matters I have had such experience as induces me to place confidence in their assertions—that by enacting certain processes, which to us moderns have something of a barbaric complexion, a very remarkable enlightenment of the spiritual faculties in man may be attained: that, for example, by absorbing the personalities of a certain number of his fellow-creatures, an individual may gain a complete ascendancy over those orders of spiritual beings which control the elemental forces of our universe.

"It is recorded of Simon Magus that he was able to fly in the air, to become invisible, or to assume any form he pleased, by the agency of the soul of a boy whom, to use the libellous phrase employed by the author of the *Clementine Recognitions,* he had 'murdered.' I find it set down, moreover, with considerable detail in the writings of Hermes Trismegistus, that similar happy results may be produced by the absorption of the hearts of not less than three human beings below the age of twenty-one years. To the testing of the truth of this receipt I have devoted the greater part of the last twenty years, selecting as the *corpora vilia* of my experiment such persons as could conveniently be removed without occasioning a sensible gap in society. The first step I effected by the removal of one Phoebe Stanley, a girl of gipsy extraction, on March 24, 1792. The second, by the removal of a wandering Italian lad, named Giovanni Paoli, on the night of March 23, 1805. The final 'victim'—to employ a word repugnant in the highest degree to my feelings—must be my cousin, Stephen Elliott. His day must be this March 24, 1812.

"The best means of effecting the required absorption is to remove the heart from the *living* subject, to reduce it to ashes, and to mingle them with about a pint of some red wine, preferably port. The remains of the first two subjects, at least, it will be well to conceal: a disused bathroom or wine-cellar will be found convenient for such a purpose. Some annoyance may be experienced from the psychic portion of the subjects, which popular language dignifies with the name of ghosts. But the man of philosophic temperament—to whom alone the experiment is appropriate—will be little prone to attach importance to the feeble efforts of these beings to wreak their vengeance on him. I contemplate with the liveliest satisfaction the enlarged and emancipated existence which the experiment, if successful, will confer on me; not only placing me beyond the reach of human justice (so-called), but eliminating to a great extent the prospect of death itself."

Mr. Abney was found in his chair, his head thrown back, his face stamped with an expression of rage, fright, and mortal pain. In his left side was a terrible lacerated wound, exposing the heart. There was no blood on his hands, and a long knife that lay on the table was perfectly clean. A savage wild-cat might have inflicted the injuries. The window of the study was open, and it was the opinion of the coroner that Mr. Abney had met his death by the agency of some wild creature. But Stephen Elliott's study of the papers I have quoted led him to a very different conclusion.

QUIET VISITORS

What of the ghost who does not come out of evil, who means no harm but seeks instead to gain sympathy from the beholder, or else to cling to a once loved home? The gentle ghost is not unknown in these tales, either, and it is fitting that such sometimes be children, or young maids caught in a shadowy half-time that is not quite of our own world.

A LITTLE GHOST

Hugh Walpole

I

GHOSTS? I looked across the table at Truscott and had a
sudden desire to impress him. Truscott has, before now,
invited confidences in just that same way, with his flat impas-
sivity, his air of not caring whether you say anything to him
or no, his determined indifference to your drama and your
pathos. On this particular evening he had been less impas-
sive. He had himself turned the conversation toward Spirit-
ualism, seances, and all that world of humbug, as he believed
it to be, and suddenly I saw, or fancied that I saw, a real
invitation in his eyes, something that made me say to myself:
"Well, hang it all, I've known Truscott for nearly twenty
years; I've never shown him the least little bit of my real self;
he thinks me a writing money-machine, with no thought in
the world beside my brazen serial stories and the yacht that I
purchased out of them."

So I told him this story, and I will do him the justice to say
that he listened to every word of it most attentively, although
it was far into the evening before I had finished. He didn't
seem impatient with all the little details that I gave. Of
course, in a ghost story, details are more important than
anything else. But was it a ghost story? Was it a story at all?
Was it true even in its material background? Now, as I try to
tell it again, I can't be sure. Truscott is the only other person
who has ever heard it, and at the end of it he made no
comment whatever.

It happened long ago, long before the War, when I had been married for about five years, and was an exceedingly prosperous journalist, with a nice little house and two children, in Wimbledon.

I lost suddenly my greatest friend. That may mean little or much as friendship is commonly held, but I believe that most Britishers, most Americans, most Scandinavians, know before they die one friendship at least that changes their whole life experience by its depth and colour. Very few Frenchmen, Italians, or Spaniards, very few Southern people at all, understand these things.

The curious part of it in my particular case was that I had known this friend only four or five years before his death, that I had made many friendships both before and since that have endured over much longer periods, and yet this particular friendship had a quality of intensity and happiness that I have never found elsewhere.

Another curious thing was that I met Bond only a few months before my marriage, when I was deeply in love with my wife, and so intensely preoccupied with my engagement that I could think of nothing else. I met Bond quite casually at someone's house. He was a large-boned, broad-shouldered, slow-smiling man with close-cropped hair turning slightly grey, and our meeting was casual; the ripening of our friendship was casual; indeed, the whole affair may be said to have been casual to the very last. It was, in fact, my wife who said to me one day, when we had been married about a year or so: "Why, I believe you care more for Charlie Bond than for anyone else in the world." She said it in that sudden, disconcerting, perceptive way that some women have. I was entirely astonished. Of course I laughed at the idea. I saw Bond frequently. He came often to the house. My wife, wiser than many wives, encouraged all my friendships, and she herself liked Charlie immensely. I don't suppose that anyone disliked him. Some men were jealous of him; some men, the merest acquaintances, called him conceited; women were sometimes irritated by him because so clearly he could get on very easily without them; but he had, I think, no real enemy.

How could he have had? His good nature, his freedom from all jealousy, his naturalness, his sense of fun, the absence of all pettiness, his common sense, his manliness, and at the same time his broad-minded intelligence, all these things made him a most charming personality. I don't know that he shone very much in ordinary society. He was very quiet and his wit and humour came out best with his intimates.

I was the showy one, and he always played up to me, and I think I patronized him a little and thought deep down in my subconscious self that it was lucky for him to have such a brilliant friend, but he never gave a sign of resentment. I believe now that he knew me, with all my faults and vanities and absurdities, far better than anyone else, even my wife, did, and that is one of the reasons, to the day of my death, why I shall always miss him so desperately.

However, it was not until his death that I realized how close we had been. One November day he came back to his flat, wet and chilled, didn't change his clothes, caught a cold, which developed into pneumonia, and after three days was dead. It happened that that week I was in Paris, and I returned to be told on my doorstep by my wife of what had occurred. At first I refused to believe it. When I had seen him a week before he had been in splendid health; with his tanned, rather rough and clumsy face, his clear eyes, no fat about him anywhere, he had looked as though he would live to a thousand, and then when I realized that it was indeed true I did not during the first week or two grasp my loss.

I missed him, of course; was vaguely unhappy and discontented; railed against life, wondering why it was always the best people who were taken and the others left; but I was not actually aware that for the rest of my days things would be different, and that that day of my return from Paris was a crisis in my human experience. Suddenly one morning, walking down Fleet Street, I had a flashing, almost blinding, need of Bond that was like a revelation. From that moment I knew no peace. Everyone seemed to me dull, profitless, and empty. Even my wife was a long way away from me, and my children, whom I dearly loved, counted nothing to me at all. I

didn't, after that, know what was the matter with me. I lost
my appetite, I couldn't sleep, I was grumpy and nervous. I
didn't myself connect it with Bond at all. I thought that I was
overworked, and when my wife suggested a holiday, I agreed,
got a fortnight's leave from my newspaper, and went down to
Glebeshire.

Early December is not a bad time for Glebeshire, it is just
then the best spot in the British Isles. I knew a little village
beyond St. Mary's Moor, that I had not seen for ten years, but
always remembered with romantic gratitude, and I felt that
that was the place for me now.

I changed trains at Polchester and found myself at last in a
little jingle driving out to sea. The air, the wide open moor,
the smell of the sea delighted me, and when I reached my
little village, with its sandy cove and the boats drawn up in
two rows in front of a high rocky cave, and when I ate my
eggs and bacon in the little parlour of the inn overlooking
the sea, I felt happier than I had done for weeks past; but my
happiness did not last long. Night after night I could not
sleep. I began to feel acute loneliness and knew at last in full
truth that it was my friend whom I was missing, and that it
was not solitude I needed, but his company. Easy enough to
talk about having his company, but I only truly knew, down
here in this little village, sitting on the edge of the green cliff,
looking over into limitless sea, that I was indeed never to
have his company again. There followed after that a wild,
impatient regret that I had not made more of my time with
him. I saw myself, in a sudden vision, as I had really been
with him, patronizing, indulgent, a little contemptuous of his
good-natured ideas. Had I only a week with him now, how
eagerly I would show him that I was the fool and not he, that
I was the lucky one every time!

One connects with one's own grief the place where one feels
it, and before many days had passed I had grown to loathe the
little village, to dread, beyond words, the long, soughing
groan of the sea as it drew back down the slanting beach, the
melancholy wail of the seagull, the chattering women under

my little window. I couldn't stand it. I ought to go back to London, and yet from that, too, I shrank. Memories of Bond lingered there as they did in no other place, and it was hardly fair to my wife and family to give them the company of the dreary, discontented man that I just then was.

And then, just in the way that such things always happen, I found on my breakfast-table one fine morning a forwarded letter. It was from a certain Mrs. Baldwin, and, to my surprise, I saw that it came from Glebeshire, but from the top of the county and not its southern end.

John Baldwin was a Stock Exchange friend of my brother's, a rough diamond, but kindly and generous, and not, I believed, very well off. Mrs. Baldwin I had always liked, and I think she always liked me. We had not met for some little time and I had no idea what had happened to them. Now in her letter she told me that they had taken an old eighteenth-century house on the north coast of Glebeshire, not very far from Drymouth, that they were enjoying it very much indeed, that Jack was fitter than he had been for years, and that they would be delighted, were I ever in that part of the country, to have me as their guest. This suddenly seemed to me the very thing. The Baldwins had never known Charlie Bond, and they would have, therefore, for me no association with his memory. They were jolly, noisy people, with a jolly, noisy family, and Jack Baldwin's personality was so robust that it would surely shake me out of my gloomy mood. I sent a telegram at once to Mrs. Baldwin, asking her whether she could have me for a week, and before the day was over I received the warmest of invitations.

Next day I left my little fishing village and experienced one of those strange, crooked, in-and-out little journeys that you must undergo if you are to find your way from one obscure Glebeshire village to another.

About midday, a lovely, cold, blue December midday, I discovered myself in Polchester with an hour to wait for my next train. I went down into the town, climbed the High

Street to the magnificent cathedral, stood beneath the famous Arden Gate, looked at the still more famous tomb of the Black Bishop, and it was there, as the sunlight, slanting through the great east window, danced and sparkled about the wonderful blue stone of which that tomb is made, that I had a sudden sense of having been through all this before, of having stood just there in some earlier time, weighed down by some earlier grief, and that nothing that I was experiencing was unexpected. I had a curious sense, too, of comfort and condolence, that horrible grey loneliness that I had felt in the fishing village suddenly fell from me, and for the first time since Bond's death, I was happy. I walked away from the cathedral, down the busy street, and through the dear old market-place, expecting I know not what. All that I knew was that I was intending to go to the Baldwin's and that I would be happy there.

The December afternoon fell quickly, and during the last part of my journey I was travelling in a ridiculous little train, through dusk, and the little train went so slowly and so casually that one was always hearing the murmur of streams beyond one's window, and lakes of grey water suddenly stretched like plates of glass to thick woods, black as ink, against a faint sky. I got out at my little wayside station, shaped like a rabbit-hutch, and found a motor waiting for me. The drive was not long, and suddenly I was outside the old eighteenth-century house and Baldwin's stout butler was conveying me into the hall with that careful, kindly patronage, rather as though I were a box of eggs that might very easily be broken.

It was a spacious hall, with a large open fireplace, in front of which they were all having tea. I say "all" advisedly, because the place seemed to be full of people, grown-ups and children, but mostly children. There were so many of these last that I was not, to the end of my stay, to be able to name most of them individually.

Mrs. Baldwin came forward to greet me, introduced me to one or two people, sat me down and gave me my tea, told me that I wasn't looking at all well, and needed feeding up, and explained that Jack was out shooting something, but would soon be back.

My entrance had made a brief lull, but immediately everyone recovered and the noise was terrific. There is a lot to be said for the freedom of the modern child. There is a lot to be said against it, too. I soon found that in this party, at any rate, the elders were completely disregarded and of no account. Children rushed about the hall, knocked one another down, shouted and screamed, fell over grown-ups as though they were pieces of furniture, and paid no attention at all to the mild "Now children" of a plain, elderly lady who was, I supposed, a governess. I fancy that I was tired with my criss-cross journey, and I soon found a chance to ask Mrs. Baldwin if I could go up to my room. She said: "I expect you find these children noisy. Poor little things. They must have their fun. Jack always says that one can only be young once, and I do so agree with him."

I wasn't myself feeling very young that evening (I was really about nine hundred years old), so that I agreed with her and eagerly left youth to its own appropriate pleasures. Mrs. Baldwin took me up the fine broad staircase. She was a stout, short woman, dressed in bright colours, with what is known, I believe, as an infectious laugh. To-night, although I was fond of her, and knew very well her good, generous heart, she irritated me, and for some reason that I could not quite define. Perhaps I felt at once that she was out of place there and that the house resented her, but in all this account, I am puzzled by the question as to whether I imagine now, on looking back, all sorts of feelings that were not really there at all, but come to me now because I know of what happened afterwards. But I am so anxious to tell the truth, the whole truth, and nothing but the truth, and there is nothing in the world so difficult to do as that.

We went through a number of dark passages, up and down little pieces of staircase that seemed to have no beginning, no end, and no reason for their existence, and she left me at last in my bedroom, said that she hoped I would be comfortable, and that Jack would come and see me when he came in, and then paused for a moment, looking at me. "You really don't look well," she said. "You've been overdoing it. You're too conscientious. I always said so. You shall have a real rest here. And the children will see that you're not dull."

Her last two sentences seemed scarcely to go together. I could not tell her about my loss. I realized suddenly, as I had never realized in our older acquaintance, that I should never be able to speak to her about anything that really mattered.

She smiled, laughed, and left me. I looked at my room and loved it at once. Broad and low-ceilinged, it contained very little furniture, an old four-poster, charming hangings of some old rose-coloured damask, an old gold mirror, an oak cabinet, some high-backed chairs, and then, for comfort, a large armchair with high elbows, a little quaintly shaped sofa dressed in the same rose colour as the bed, a bright crackling fire, and a grandfather clock. The walls, faded primrose, had no pictures, but on one of them, opposite my bed, was a gay sampler worked in bright colours of crimson and yellow and framed in oak.

I liked it, I loved it, and drew the armchair in front of the fire, nestled down into it, and before I knew, I was fast asleep. How long I slept I don't know, but I suddenly woke with a sense of comfort and well-being which was nothing less than exquisite. I belonged to it, that room, as though I had been in it all my days. I had a curious sense of companionship that was exactly what I had been needing during these last weeks. The house was very still, no voices of children came to me, no sound anywhere, save the sharp crackle of the fire and the friendly ticking of the old clock. Suddenly I thought that there was someone in the room with me, a rustle of something that might have been the fire and yet was not.

I got up and looked about me, half smiling, as though I expected to see a familiar face. There was no one there, of course, and yet I had just that consciousness of companionship that one has when someone whom one loves very dearly and knows very intimately is sitting with one in the same room. I even went to the other side of the four-poster and looked around me, pulled for a moment at the silver-coloured curtains, and of course saw no one. Then the door suddenly opened and Jack Baldwin came in, and I remember having a curious feeling of irritation as though I had been interrupted. His large, breezy, knickerbockered figure filled the room. "Hullo!" he said, "delighted to see you. Bit of luck your being down this way. Have you got everything you want?"

II

That was a wonderful old house. I am not going to attempt to describe it, although I have stayed there quite recently. Yes, I stayed there on many occasions since that first of which I am now speaking. It has never been quite the same to me since that first time. You may say, if you like, that the Baldwins fought a battle with it and defeated it. It is certainly now more Baldwin than—well, whatever it was before they rented it. They are not the kind of people to be defeated by atmosphere. Their chief duty in this world, I gather, is to make things Baldwin, and very good for the world too; but when I first went down to them the house was still challenging them. "A wee bit creepy," Mrs. Baldwin confided to me on the second day of my visit. "What exactly do you mean by that?" I asked her. "Ghosts?"

"Oh, there are those, of course," she answered. "There's an underground passage, you know, that runs from here to the sea, and one of the wickedest of the smugglers was killed in it, and his ghost still haunts the cellar. At least that's what we were told by our first butler, here; and then, of course, we found that it was the butler, not the smuggler, who was haunting the cellar, and since his departure the smuggler hasn't been visible." She laughed. "All the same, it isn't a comfortable place. I'm going to wake up some of those old rooms. We're going to put in some more windows. And then there are the children," she added.

Yes, there were the children. Surely the noisiest in all the world. They had reverence for nothing. They were the wildest savages, and especially those from nine to thirteen, the cruellest and most uncivilized age for children. There were two little boys, twins I should think, who were nothing less than devils, and regarded their elders with cold, watching eyes, said nothing in protest when scolded, but evolved plots afterwards that fitted precisely the chastiser. To do my host and hostess justice, all the children were not Baldwins, and I fancy that the Baldwin contingent was the quietest.

Nevertheless, from early morning until ten at night, the noise was terrific and you were never sure how early in the morning it would recommence. I don't know that I personally minded the noise very greatly. It took me out of myself and gave me something better to think of, but, in some obscure and unanalysed way, I felt that the house minded it. One knows how the poets have written about old walls and rafters rejoicing in the happy, careless laughter of children. I do not think this house rejoiced at all, and it was queer how consistently I, who am not supposed to be an imaginative person, thought about the house.

But it was not until my third evening that something really happened. I say "happened," but did anything really happen? You shall judge for yourself.

I was sitting in my comfortable armchair in my bedroom, enjoying that delightful half-hour before one dresses for dinner. There was a terrible racket up and down the passages, the children being persuaded, I gathered, to go into the schoolroom and have their supper, when the noise died down and there was nothing but the feathery whisper of the snow—snow had been falling all day—against my window-pane. My thoughts suddenly turned to Bond, directed to him as actually and precipitately as though he had suddenly sprung before me. I did not want to talk of him. I had been fighting his memory these last days, because I had thought that the wisest thing to do, but now he was too much for me.

I luxuriated in my memories of him, turning over and over all sorts of times that we had had together, seeing his smile, watching his mouth that turned up at the corners when he was amused, and wondering finally why he should obsess me the way that he did, when I had lost so many other friends for whom I had thought I cared much more, who, nevertheless, never bothered my memory at all. I sighed, and it seemed to me that my sigh was very gently repeated behind me. I turned sharply round. The curtains had not been drawn. You know the strange, milky pallor that reflected snow throws over objects, and although three lighted candles shone in the room, moon-white shadows seemed to hang over the bed and across the floor. Of course there was no one there, and yet I stared and stared about me as though I were convinced that I was not alone. And then I looked especially at one part of the room, a distant corner beyond the four-poster, and it seemed to me that someone was there. And yet no one was there. But whether it was that my mind had been distracted, or that the beauty of the old snow-lit room enchanted me, I don't know, but my thoughts of my friend were happy and reassured. I had not lost him, I seemed to say to myself. Indeed, at that special moment he seemed to be closer to me than he had been while he was alive.

From that evening a curious thing occurred. I only seemed to be close to my friend when I was in my own room—and I felt more than that. When my door was closed and I was sitting in my armchair, I fancied that our new companion-ship was not only Bond's, but was something more as well. I would wake in the middle of the night or in the early morning and feel quite sure that I was not alone; so sure that I did not even want to investigate it further, but just took the companionship for granted and was happy.

Outside that room, however, I felt increasing discomfort. I hated the way in which the house was treated. A quite unreasonable anger rose within me as I heard the Baldwins discussing the improvements that they were going to make, and yet they were so kind to me, and so patently unaware of doing anything that would not generally be commended, that it was quite impossible for me to show my anger. Neverthe-less, Mrs. Baldwin noticed something. "I am afraid the chil-dren are worrying you," she said one morning, half interrogatively. "In a way it will be a rest when they go back to school, but the Christmas holidays is their time, isn't it? I do like to see them happy. Poor little dears."

The poor little dears were at that moment being Red Indians all over the hall.

"No, of course, I like children," I answered her. "The only thing is that they don't—I hope you won't think me foolish—somehow quite fit in with the house."

"Oh, I think it's so good for old places like this," said Mrs. Baldwin briskly, "to be woken up a little. I'm sure if the old people who used to live here came back they'd love to hear all the noise and laughter."

I wasn't so sure myself, but I wouldn't disturb Mrs. Baldwin's contentment for anything.

That evening in my room I was so convinced of companionship that I spoke.

"If there's anyone here," I said aloud, "I'd like them to know that I'm aware of it and am glad of it."

Then, when I caught myself speaking aloud, I was suddenly terrified. Was I really going crazy? Wasn't that the first step towards insanity when you talked to yourself? Nevertheless, a moment later I was reassured. There *was* someone there.

That night I woke, looked at my luminous watch and saw that it was a quarter past three. The room was so dark that I could not even distinguish the posters of my bed, but—there was a very faint glow from the fire, now nearly dead. Opposite my bed there seemed to me to be something white. Not white in the accepted sense of a tall, ghostly figure; but, sitting up and staring, it seemed to me that the shadow was very small, hardly reaching above the edge of the bed.

"Is there anyone there?" I asked. "Because, if there is, do speak to me. I'm not frightened. I know that someone has been here all this last week, and I am glad of it."

Very faintly then, and so faintly that I cannot to this day be sure that I saw anything at all, the figure of a child seemed to me to be visible.

We all know how we have at one time and another fancied that we have seen visions and figures, and then have discovered that it was something in the room, the chance hanging of a coat, the reflection of a glass, a trick of moonlight that has fired our imagination. I was quite prepared for that in this case, but it seemed to me then that as I watched the shadow moved directly in front of the dying fire, and delicate as the leaf of a silver birch, like the trailing rim of some evening cloud, the figure of a child hovered in front of me.

Curiously enough the dress, which seemed to be of some silver tissue, was clearer than anything else. I did not, in fact, see the face at all, and yet I could swear in the morning that I had seen it, that I knew large, black, wide-open eyes, a little mouth very faintly parted in a timid smile, and that, beyond anything else, I had realized in the expression of that face fear and bewilderment and a longing for some comfort.

III

After that night the affair moved very quickly to its little climax.

I am not a very imaginative man, nor have I any sympathy with the modern craze for spooks and spectres. I have never seen, nor fancied that I had seen, anything of a supernatural kind since that visit, but then I have never known since that time such a desperate need of companionship and comfort, and is it not perhaps because we do not want things badly enough in this life that we do not get more of them? However that may be, I was sure on this occasion that I had some companionship that was born of a need greater than mine. I suddenly took the most frantic and unreasonable dislike of the children in that house. It was exactly as though I had discovered somewhere in a deserted part of the building some child who had been left behind by mistake by the last occupants and was terrified by the noisy exuberance and ruthless selfishness of the new family.

For a week I had no more definite manifestation of my little friend, but I was as sure of her presence there in my room as I was of my own clothes and the armchair in which I used to sit.

It was time for me to go back to London, but I could not go. I asked everyone I met as to legends and stories connected with the old house, but I never found anything to do with a little child. I looked forward all day to my hour in my room before dinner, the time when I felt the companionship closest. I sometimes woke in the night and was conscious of its presence, but, as I have said, I never saw anything.

One evening the older children obtained leave to stay up later. It was somebody's birthday. The house seemed to be full of people, and the presence of the children led after dinner to a perfect riot of noise and confusion. We were to play hide-and-seek all over the house. Everybody was to dress up. There was, for that night at least, to be no privacy anywhere. We were all, as Mrs. Baldwin said, to be ten years old again. I hadn't the least desire to be ten years old, but I found myself caught into the game, and had, in sheer self-defence, to run up and down the passages and hide behind doors. The noise was terrific. It grew and grew in volume. People got hysterical. The smaller children jumped out of bed and ran about the passages. Somebody kept blowing a motor-horn. Somebody else turned on the gramophone.

Suddenly I was sick of the whole thing, retreated into my room, lit one candle, and locked the door. I had scarcely sat down in my chair when I was aware that my little friend had come. She was standing near to the bed, staring at me, terror in her eyes. I have never seen anyone so frightened. Her little breasts panting beneath her silver gown, her very fair hair falling about her shoulders, her little hands clenched. Just as I saw her, there were loud knocks on the door, many voices shouting to be admitted, a perfect babel of noise and laughter. The little figure moved, and then—how can I give any idea of it?—I was conscious of having something to protect and comfort. I saw nothing, physically I felt nothing, and yet I was murmuring, "There, there, don't mind. They shan't come in. I'll see that no one touches you. I understand. I understand." For how long I sat like that I don't know. The noises died away, voices murmured at intervals, and then were silent. The house slept. All night I think I stayed there comforting and being comforted.

I fancy now—but how much of it may not be fancy?—that I knew that the child loved the house, had stayed so long as was possible, at last was driven away, and that that was her farewell, not only to me, but all that she most loved in this world and the next.

I do not know—I could swear to nothing. Of what I am sure is that my sense of loss in my friend was removed from that night and never returned. Did I argue with myself that that child companionship included also my friend? Again, I do not know. But of one thing I am now sure, that if love is strong enough, physical death cannot destroy it, and however platitudinous that may sound to others, it is platitudinous no longer when you have discovered it by actual experience for yourself.

That moment in that fire-lit room, when I felt that spiritual heart beating with mine, is and always will be enough for me.

One thing more. Next day I left for London, and my wife was delighted to find me so completely recovered—happier, she said, than I had ever been before.

Two days afterwards, I received a parcel from Mrs. Baldwin. In the note that accompanied it, she said:

> I think that you must have left this by mistake behind you. It was found in the small drawer in your dressing-table.

I opened the parcel and discovered an old blue silk handkerchief, wrapped round a long, thin wooden box. The cover of the box lifted very easily, and I saw inside it an old, painted wooden doll, dressed in the period, I should think, of Queen Anne. The dress was very complete, even down to the little shoes, and the little grey mittens on the hands. Inside the silk skirt there was sewn a little tape, and on the tape, in very faded letters, "Ann Trelawney, 1710."

PLAYMATES

A. M. Burrage

I

ALTHOUGH everybody who knew Stephen Everton agreed
that he was the last man under Heaven who ought to have
been allowed to bring up a child, it was fortunate for Monica
that she fell into his hands; else she had probably starved or
drifted into some refuge for waifs and strays. True her father,
Sebastian Threlfall the poet, had plenty of casual friends.
Almost everybody knew him slightly, and right up to the
time of his fatal attack of *delirium tremens* he contrived to
look one of the most interesting of the regular frequenters of
the Café Royal. But people are generally not hasty to bring
up the children of casual acquaintances, particularly when
such children may be suspected of having inherited more
than a fair share of human weaknesses.

Of Monica's mother literally nothing was known. Nobody
seemed able to say if she were dead or alive. Probably she had
long since deserted Threlfall for some consort able and
willing to provide regular meals.

Everton knew Threlfall no better than a hundred others
knew him, and was ignorant of his daughter's existence until
the father's death was a new topic of conversation in literary
and artistic circles. People vaguely wondered what would
become of "the kid"; and while they were still wondering,
Everton quietly took possession of her.

Who's Who will tell you the year of Everton's birth, the
names of his *Almae Matres* (Winchester and Magdalen Col-

lege, Oxford), the titles of his books and of his predilections
for skating and mountaineering; but it is necessary to know
the man a little less superficially. He was then a year or two
short of fifty and looked ten years older. He was a tall, lean
man, with a delicate pink complexion, an oval head, a
Roman nose, blue eyes which looked out mildly through
strong glasses, and thin straight lips drawn tightly over
slightly protruding teeth. His high forehead was bare, for he
was bald to the base of his skull. What remained of his hair
was a neutral tint between black and grey, and was kept
closely cropped. He contrived to look at once prim and
irascible, scholarly and acute; Sherlock Holmes, perhaps,
with a touch of old-maidishness.

The world knew him for a writer of books on historical
crises. They were cumbersome books with cumbersome titles,
written by a scholar for scholars. They brought him fame and
not a little money. The money he could have afforded to be
without, since he was modestly wealthy by inheritance. He
was essentially a cold-blooded animal, a bachelor, a man of
regular and temperate habits, fastidious, and fond of qui-
etude and simple comforts.

Nobody is ever likely to know why Everton adopted the
orphan daughter of a man whom he knew but slightly and
neither liked nor respected. He was no lover of children, and
his humours were sardonic rather than sentimental. I am
only hazarding a guess when I suggest that, like so many
childless men, he had theories of his own concerning the
upbringing of children, which he wanted to see tested. Certain it is that Monica's childhood, which had been extraordinary enough before, passed from the tragic to the grotesque.

Everton took Monica from the Bloomsbury "apartments"
house, where the landlady, already nursing a bad debt, was
wondering how to dispose of the child. Monica was then
eight years old, and a woman of the world in her small way.
She had lived with drink and poverty and squalor; had never
played a game nor had a playmate; had seen nothing but the
seamy side of life; and had learned skill in practising her
father's petty shifts and mean contrivances. She was grave and

sullen and plain and pale, this child who had never known childhood. When she spoke, which was as seldom as possible, her voice was hard and gruff. She was, poor little thing, as unattractive as her life could have made her.

She went with Everton without question or demur. She would no more have questioned anybody's ownership than if she had been an inanimate piece of luggage left in a cloak-room. She had belonged to her father. Now that he was gone to his own place she was the property of whomsoever chose to claim her. Everton took her with a cold kindness in which was neither love nor pity; in return she gave him neither love nor gratitude, but did as she was desired after the manner of a paid servant.

Everton disliked modern children, and for what he dis-liked in them he blamed modern schools. It may have been on this account that he did not send Monica to one; or perhaps he wanted to see how a child would contrive its own education. Monica could already read and write and, thus equipped, she had the run of his large library, in which was almost every conceivable kind of book from heavy tomes on abstruse subjects to trashy modern novels bought and left there by Miss Gribbin. Everton barred nothing, recom-mended nothing, but watched the tree grow naturally, un-tended and unpruned.

Miss Gribbin was Everton's secretary. She was the kind of hatchet-faced, flat-chested, middle-aged sexless woman who could safely share the home of a bachelor without either of them being troubled by the tongue of Scandal. To her duties was now added the instruction of Monica in certain ele-mentary subjects. Thus Monica learned that a man named William the Conqueror arrived in England in 1066; but to find out what manner of man this William was, she had to go to the library and read the conflicting accounts of him given by the several historians. From Miss Gribbin she learned bare irrefutable facts; for the rest she was left to fend for herself. In the library she found herself surrounded by all the realms of reality and fancy, each with its door invitingly ajar.

Monica was fond of reading. It was, indeed, almost her only recreation, for Everton knew no other children of her age, and treated her as a grown-up member of the household. Thus she read everything from translations of the *Iliad* to Hans Andersen, from the Bible to the love-gush of the modern female fictionmongers.

Everton, although he watched her closely, and plied her with innocent-sounding questions, was never allowed a peep into her mind. What muddled dreams she may have had of a strange world surrounding the Hampstead house—a world of gods and fairies and demons, and strong silent men making love to sloppy-minded young women—she kept to herself. Reticence was all that she had in common with normal childhood, and Everton noticed that she never played.

Unlike most young animals, she did not take naturally to playing. Perhaps the instinct had been beaten out of her by the realities of life while her father was alive. Most lonely children improvise their own games and provide themselves with a vast store of make-believe. But Monica, as sullen-seeming as a caged animal, devoid alike of the naughtiness and the charms of childhood, rarely crying and still more rarely laughing, moved about the house sedate to the verge of being wooden. Occasionally Everton, the experimentalist, had twinges of conscience and grew half afraid. . . .

II

When Monica was twelve Everton moved his establishment from Hampstead to a house remotely situated in the middle of Suffolk, which was part of a recent legacy. It was a tall, rectangular, Queen Anne house standing on a knoll above marshy fields and wind-bowed beech woods. Once it had been the manor house, but now little land went with it. A short drive passed between rank evergreens from the heavy wrought-iron gate to a circle of grass and flower beds in front of the house. Behind was an acre and a half of rank garden, given over to weeds and marigolds. The rooms were high and well lighted, but the house wore an air of depression as if it were a live thing unable to shake off some ancient fit of melancholy.

Everton went to live in the house for a variety of reasons. For the most part of a year he had been trying in vain to let or sell it, and it was when he found that he would have no difficulty in disposing of his house at Hampstead that he made up his mind. The old house, a mile distant from a remote Suffolk village, would give him all the solitude he required. Moreover he was anxious about his health—his nervous system had never been strong—and his doctor had recommended the bracing air of East Anglia.

He was not in the least concerned to find that the house was too big for him. His furniture filled the same number of rooms as it had filled at Hampstead, and the others he left empty. Nor did he increase his staff of three indoor servants and gardener. Miss Gribbin, now less dispensable than ever, accompanied him; and with them came Monica to see another aspect of life, with the same wooden stoicism which Everton had remarked in her upon the occasion of their first meeting.

As regarded Monica, Miss Gribbin's duties were then becoming more and more of a sinecure. "Lessons" now occupied no more than half an hour a day. The older Monica grew, the better she was able to grub for her education in the great library. Between Monica and Miss Gribbin there was neither love nor sympathy, nor was there any affectation of either. In their common duty to Everton they owed and paid certain duties to each other. Their intercourse began and ended there.

Everton and Miss Gribbin both liked the house at first. It suited the two temperaments which were alike in their lack of festivity. Asked if she too liked it, Monica said simply "Yes," in a tone which implied stolid and complete indifference.

All three in their several ways led much the same lives as they had led at Hampstead. But a slow change began to work in Monica, a change so slight and subtle that weeks passed before Everton or Miss Gribbin noticed it. It was late on an afternoon in early spring when Everton first became aware of something unusual in Monica's demeanor.

He had been searching in the library for one of his own books—*The Fall of the Commonwealth of England*—and having failed to find it went in search of Miss Gribbin and met Monica instead at the foot of the long oak staircase. Of her he casually inquired about the book, and she jerked up her head brightly, to answer him with an unwonted smile:

"Yes, I've been reading it. I expect I left it in the schoolroom. I'll go and see."

It was a long speech for her to have uttered, but Everton scarcely noticed that at the time. His attention was directed elsewhere.

"*Where* did you leave it?" he demanded.

"In the schoolroom," she repeated.

"I know of no schoolroom," said Everton coldly. He hated to hear anything mis-called, even were it only a room. "Miss Gribbin generally takes you for your lessons in either the library or the dining-room. If it is one of those rooms, kindly call it by its proper name."

Monica shook her head.

"No, I mean the schoolroom—the big empty room next to the library. That's what it's called."

Everton knew the room. It faced north, and seemed darker and more dismal than any other room in the house. He had wondered idly why Monica chose to spend so much of her time in a room bare of furniture, with nothing better to sit on then uncovered boards or a cushionless window-seat; and put it down to her genius for being unlike anybody else.

"Who calls it that?" he demanded.

"*It's* its name," said Monica smiling.

She ran upstairs, and presently returned with the book, which she handed to him with another smile. He was already wondering at her. It was surprising and pleasant to see her run, instead of the heavy and clumsy walk which generally moved her when she went to obey a behest. And she had smiled two or three times in the short space of a minute.

Then he realized that for some little while she had been a brighter, happier creature than she had ever been at Hampstead.

"How did you come to call that room the schoolroom?" he asked, as he took the book from her hand.

"It *is* the schoolroom," she insisted, seeking to cover her evasion by laying stress on the verb.

That was all he could get out of her. As he questioned further the smiles ceased and the pale, plain little face became devoid of any expression. He knew then that it was useless to press her, but his curiosity was aroused. He inquired of Miss Gribbin and the servant, and learned that nobody was in the habit of calling the long, empty apartment the schoolroom.

Clearly Monica had given it its name. But why? She was so altogether remote from school and schoolrooms. Some germ of imagination was active in her small mind. Everton's interest was stimulated. He was like a doctor who remarks in a patient some abnormal symptom.

"Monica seems a lot brighter and more alert than she used to be," he remarked to Miss Gribbin.

"Yes," agreed the secretary. "I have noticed that. She is learning to play.'"

"To play what? The piano?"

"No, no. To play childish games. Haven't you heard her dancing about and singing?"

Everton shook his head and looked interested.

"I have not," he said. "Possibly my presence acts as a check upon her—er—exuberance."

"I hear her in that empty room which she insists upon calling the schoolroom. She stops when she hears my step. Of course, I have not interfered with her in any way, but I could wish that she would not talk to herself. I don't like people who do that. It is somehow—uncomfortable."

"I didn't know she did," said Everton slowly.

"Oh, yes, quite long conversations. I haven't actually heard what she talks about, but sometimes you would think she was in the midst of a circle of friends."

"In that same room?"

"Generally," said Miss Gribbin, with a nod.

Everton regarded his secretary with a slow, thoughtful smile.

"Development," he said, "is always extremely interesting. I am glad the place seems to suit Monica. I think it suits all of us."

There was a doubtful note in his voice as he uttered the last words, and Miss Gribbin agreed with him with the same lack of conviction in her tone. As a fact, Everton had been doubtful of late if his health had been benefited by the move from Hampstead. For the first week or two his nerves had been the better for the change of air; but now he was conscious of the beginning of a relapse. His imagination was beginning to play him tricks, filling his mind with vague, distorted fancies. Sometimes when he sat up late, writing—he was given to working at night on strong coffee—he became a victim of the most distressing nervous symptoms, hard to analyze and impossible to combat, which invariably drove him to bed with a sense of defeat.

That same night he suffered one of the variations of this common experience.

It was close upon midnight when he felt stealing over him a sense of discomfort which he was compelled to classify as fear. He was working in a small room leading out of the drawing-room which he had selected for his study. At first he was scarcely aware of the sensation. The effect was always cumulative; the burden was laid upon him straw by straw.

It began with his being oppressed by the silence of the house. He became more and more acutely conscious of it, until it became like a thing tangible, a prison of solid walls growing around him.

The scratching of his pen at first relieved the tension. He wrote words and erased them again for the sake of that comfortable sound. But presently that comfort was denied him, for it seemed to him that this minute and busy noise was attracting attention to himself. Yes, that was it. He was being watched.

Everton sat quite still, the pen poised an inch above the half-covered sheet of paper. This was become a familiar sensation. He was being watched. And by what? And from what corner of the room?

He forced a tremulous smile to his lips. One moment he called himself ridiculous; the next, he asked himself hopelessly how a man could argue with his nerves. Experience had taught him that the only cure—and that a temporary one— was to go to bed. Yet he sat on, anxious to learn more about himself, to coax his vague imaginings into some definite shape.

Imagination told him that he was being watched, and although he called it imagination he was afraid. That rapid beating against his ribs was his heart, warning him of fear. But he sat rigid, anxious to learn in what part of the room his fancy would place these imaginary "watchers"—for he was conscious of the gaze of more than one pair of eyes being bent upon him.

At first the experiment failed. The rigidity of his pose, the hold he was keeping upon himself, acted as a brake upon his mind. Presently he realized this and relaxed the tension, striving to give his mind that perfect freedom which might have been demanded by a hypnotist or one experimenting in telepathy.

Almost at once he thought of the door. The eyes of his mind veered round in that direction as the needle of a compass veers to the magnetic north. With these eyes of his imagination he saw the door. It was standing half open, and the aperture was thronged with faces. What kind of faces he could not tell. They were just faces; imagination left it at that. But he was aware that these spies were timid; that they were in some wise as fearful of him as he was of them; that to scatter them he had but to turn his head and gaze at them with the eyes of his body.

The door was at his shoulder. He turned his head suddenly and gave it one swift glance out of the tail of his eye.

However imagination deceived him, it had not played him

false about the door. It was standing half open although he could have sworn that he had closed it on entering the room. The aperture was empty. Only darkness, solid as a pillar, filled the space between floor and lintel. But although he saw nothing as he turned his head, he was dimly conscious of something vanishing, a scurrying noiseless and incredibly swift, like the flitting of trout in clear, shallow water.

Everton stood up, stretched himself, and brought his knuckles up to his strained eyes. He told himself that he must go to bed. It was bad enough that he must suffer these nervous attacks; to encourage them was madness.

But as he mounted the stairs he was still conscious of not being alone. Shy, timorous, ready to melt into the shadows of the walls if he turned his head, *they* were following him, whispering noiselessly, linking hands and arms, watching him with the fearful, awed curiosity of—Children.

III

The Vicar had called upon Everton. His name was Parslow, and he was a typical country parson of the poorer sort, a tall, rugged, shabby, worried man in the middle forties, obviously embarrassed by the eternal problem of making ends meet on an inadequate stipend.

Everton received him courteously enough, but with a certain coldness which implied that he had nothing in common with his visitor. Parslow was evidently disappointed because "the new people" were not church-goers nor likely to take much interest in the parish. The two men made half-hearted and vain attempts to find common ground. It was not until he was on the point of leaving that the Vicar mentioned Monica.

"You have, I believe, a little girl?" he said.

"Yes. My small ward."

"Ah! I expect she finds it lonely here. I have a little girl of the same age. She is at present away at school, but she will be home soon for the Easter holidays. I know she would be delighted if your little—er—ward would come down to the Vicarage and play with her sometimes."

The suggestion was not particularly welcome to Everton, and his thanks were perfunctory. This other small girl, although she was a vicar's daughter, might carry the contagion of other modern children and infect Monica with the pertness and slanginess which he so detested. Altogether he was determined to have as little to do with the Vicarage as possible.

Meanwhile the child was becoming to him a study of more and more absorbing interest. The change in her was almost as marked as if she had just returned after having spent a term at school. She astonished and mystified him by using expressions which she could scarcely have learned from any member of the household. It was not the jargon of the smart young people of the day which slipped easily from her lips, but the polite family slang of his own youth. For instance, she remarked one morning that Mead, the gardener, was a whale at pruning vines.

A whale! The expression took Everton back a very long way down the level road of the spent years; took him, indeed, to a nursery in a solid respectable house in a Belgravian square, where he had heard the word used in that same sense for the first time. His sister Gertrude, aged ten, notorious in those days for picking up loose expressions, announced that she was getting to be a whale at French. Yes, in those days an expert was a "whale" or a "don"; not, as he is to-day, a "stout fellow." But who was a "whale" nowadays? It was years since he had heard the term.

"Where did you learn to say that?" he demanded in so strange a tone that Monica stared at him anxiously.

"Isn't it right?" she asked eagerly. She might have been a child at a new school, fearful of not having acquired the fashionable phraseology of the place.

"It is a slang expression," said the purist coldly. "It used to mean a person who was proficient in something. How did you come to hear it?"

She smiled without answering, and her smile was mysterious, even coquettish after a childish fashion. Silence had always been her refuge, but it was no longer a sullen silence. She was changing rapidly, and in a manner to bewilder her guardian. He failed in an effort to cross-examine her, and, later in the day, consulted Miss Gribbin.

"That child," he said, "is reading something that we know nothing about."

"Just at present," said Miss Gribbin, "she is glued to Dickens and Stevenson."

"Then where on earth does she get her expressions?"

"I don't know," the secretary retorted testily, "any more than I know how she learned to play Cat's Cradle."

"What? That game with string? Does she play that?"

"I found her doing something quite complicated and elaborate the other day. She wouldn't tell me how she learned to do it. I took the trouble to question the servants, but none of them had shown her."

Everton frowned.

"And I know of no book in the library which tells how to perform tricks with string. Do you think she has made a clandestine friendship with any of the village children?"

Miss Gribbin shook her head.

"She is too fastidious for that. Besides, she seldom goes into the village alone."

There, for the time, the discussion ended. Everton, with all the curiosity of the student, watched the child as carefully and closely as he was able without at the same time arousing her suspicions. She was developing fast. He had known that she must develop, but the manner of her doing so amazed and mystified him, and, likely as not, denied some preconceived theory. The untended plant was not only growing but showed signs of pruning. It was as if there were outside influences at work on Monica which could have come neither from him nor from any other member of the household.

Winter was dying hard, and dark days of rain kept Miss Gribbin, Monica, and Everton within doors. He lacked no opportunities of keeping the child under observation, and once, on a gloomy afternoon, passing the room which she had named the schoolroom, he paused and listened until he became suddenly aware that his conduct bore an unpleasant resemblance to eavesdropping. The psychologist and the gentleman engaged in a brief struggle in which the gentleman temporarily got the upper hand. Everton approached the door with a heavy step and flung it open.

The sensation he received, as he pushed open the door, was vague but slightly disturbing, and it was by no means new to him. Several times of late, but generally after dark, he had entered an empty room with the impression that it had been occupied by others until the very moment of his crossing the threshold. His coming disturbed not merely one or two, but a crowd. He felt rather than heard them scattering, flying swiftly and silently as shadows to incredible hiding-places, where they held breath and watched and waited for him to go. Into the same atmosphere of tension he now walked, and looked about him as if expecting to see more than only the child who held the floor in the middle of the room, or some tell-tale trace of other children in hiding. Had the room been furnished he must have looked involuntarily for shoes protruding from under tables or settees, for ends of garments unconsciously left exposed.

The long room, however, was empty save for Monica from wainscot to wainscot and from floor to ceiling. Fronting him were the long, high windows starred by fine rain. With her back to the white filtered light Monica faced him, looking up to him as he entered. He was just in time to see a smile fading from her lips. He also saw by a slight convulsive movement of her shoulders that she was hiding something from him in the hands clasped behind her back.

"Hullo," he said, with a kind of forced geniality, "what are you up to?"

She said: "Nothing," but not as sullenly as she would once have said it.

"Come," said Everton, "that is impossible. You were talking to yourself, Monica. You should not do that. It is an idle

and very, very foolish habit. You will go mad if you continue
to do that."

She let her head droop a little.

"I wasn't talking to myself," she said in a low, half playful
but very deliberate tone.

"That's nonsense. I heard you."

"I wasn't talking to myself."

"But you must have been. There is nobody else here."

"There isn't—now."

"What do you mean? Now?"

"They've gone. You frightened them, I expect."

"What do you mean?" he repeated, advancing a step or two
towards her. "And whom do you call 'they'?"

Next moment he was angry with himself. His tone was so
heavy and serious and the child was half laughing at him. It
was as if she were triumphant at having inveigled him into
taking a serious part in her own game of make-believe.

"You wouldn't understand," she said.

"I understand this—that you are wasting your time and
being a very silly little girl. What's that you're hiding behind
your back?"

She held out her right hand at once, unclenched her
fingers and disclosed a thimble. He looked at it and then into
her face.

"Why did you hide that from me?" he asked. "There was
no need."

She gave him a faint secretive smile—that new smile of
hers—before replying.

"We were playing with it. I didn't want you to know."

"*You* were playing with it, you mean. And why didn't you
want me to know?"

"About them. Because I thought you wouldn't understand.
You *don't* understand."

He saw that it was useless to affect anger or show impa-
tience. He spoke to her gently, even with an attempt at
displaying sympathy.

"Who are 'they'?" he asked.

"They're just them. Other girls."

"I see. And they come and play with you, do they? And they run away whenever I'm about, because they don't like me. Is that it?"

She shook her head.

"It isn't that they don't like you. I think they like everybody. But they're so shy. They were shy of me for a long, long time. I knew they were there, but it was weeks and weeks before they'd come and play with me. It was weeks before I even saw them."

"Yes? Well, what are they like?"

"Oh, they're just girls. And they're awfully, awfully nice. Some are a bit older than me and some are a bit younger. And they don't dress like other girls you see to-day. They're in white with longer skirts and they wear sashes."

Everton inclined his head gravely. "She got that out of the illustrations of books in the library," he reflected.

"You don't happen to know their names, I suppose?" he asked, hoping that no quizzical note in his voice rang through the casual but sincere tone which he intended.

"Oh, yes. There's Mary Hewitt—I think I love her best of all—and Elsie Power and—"

"How many of them altogether?"

"Seven. It's just a nice number. And this is the schoolroom where we play games. I love games. I wish I'd learned to play games before."

"And you've been playing with the thimble?"

"Yes. Hunt-the-thimble they call it. One of us hides it, and then the rest of us try to find it, and the one who finds it hides it again."

"You mean you hide it yourself, and then go and find it."

The smile left her face at once, and the look in her eyes warned him that she was done with confidences.

"Ah!" she exclaimed. "You don't understand after all. I somehow knew you wouldn't."

Everton, however, thought he did. His face wore a sudden smile of relief.

"Well, never mind," he said. "But I shouldn't play too much if I were you."

With that he left her. But curiosity tempted him, not in vain, to linger and listen for a moment on the other side of the door which he had closed behind him. He heard Monica whisper:

"Mary! Elsie! Come on. It's all right. He's gone now."

At an answering whisper, very unlike Monica's, he started violently and then found himself grinning at his own discomfiture. It was natural that Monica, playing many parts, should try to change her voice with every character. He went downstairs sunk in a brown study which brought him to certain interesting conclusions. A little later he communicated these to Miss Gribbin.

"I've discovered the cause of the change in Monica. She's invented for herself some imaginary friends—other little girls, of course."

Miss Gribbin started slightly and looked up from the newspaper which she had been reading.

"Really?" she exclaimed. "Isn't that rather an unhealthy sign?"

"No, I should say not. Having imaginary friends is quite a common symptom of childhood, especially among young girls. I remember my sister used to have one, and was very angry when none of the rest of us would take the matter seriously. In Monica's case I should say it was perfectly normal—normal, but interesting. She must have inherited an imagination from that father of hers, with the result that she has seven imaginary friends, all properly named, if you please. You see, being lonely, and having no friends of her own age, she would naturally invent more than one 'friend.' They are all nicely and primly dressed, I must tell you, out of Victorian books which she has found in the library."

"It can't be healthy," said Miss Gribbin, pursing her lips. "And I can't understand how she has learned certain expressions and a certain style of talking and games—"

"All out of books. And pretends to herself that 'they' have

taught her. But the most interesting part of the affair is this:
it's given me my first practical experience of telepathy, of the
existence of which I have hitherto been rather sceptical.
Since Monica invented this new game, and before I was
aware that she had done so, I have had at different times
distinct impressions of there being a lot of little girls about
the house."

Miss Gribbin started and stared. Her lips parted as if she
were about to speak, but it was as if she had changed her
mind while framing the first word she had been about to
utter.

"Monica," he continued smiling, "invented these 'friends,'
and has been making me telepathically aware of them, too. I
have lately been most concerned about the state of my
nerves."

Miss Gribbin jumped up as if in anger, but her brow was
smooth and her mouth dropped at the corners.

"Mr. Everton," she said, "I wish you had not told me all
this." Her lips worked. "You see," she added unsteadily, "I
don't believe in telepathy."

IV

Easter, which fell early that year, brought little Gladys
Parslow home for the holidays to the Vicarage. The event was
shortly afterwards signalized by a note from the Vicar to
Everton, inviting him to send Monica down to have tea and
play games with his little daughter on the following Wednes-
day.

The invitation was an annoyance and an embarrassment to
Everton. Here was the disturbing factor, the outside influence, which might possibly thwart his experiment in the
upbringing of Monica. He was free, of course, simply to
decline the invitation so coldly and briefly as to make sure
that it would not be repeated; but the man was not strong
enough to stand on his own feet impervious to the winds of
criticism. He was sensitive and had little wish to seem churl-

ish, still less to appear ridiculous. Taking the line of least
resistance he began to reason that one child, herself no older
than Monica, and in the atmosphere of her own home, could
make but little impression. It ended in his allowing Monica
to go.

Monica herself seemed pleased at the prospect of going but
expressed her pleasure in a discreet, restrained, grown-up
way. Miss Gribbin accompanied her as far as the Vicarage
doorstep, arriving with her punctually at half-past three on a
sullen and muggy afternoon, and handed her over to the
woman-of-all-work who answered the summons at the door.

Miss Gribbin reported to Everton on her return. An idea
which she conceived to be humorous had possession of her
mind, and in talking to Everton she uttered one of her infre-
quent laughs.

"I only left her at the door," she said, "so I didn't see her
meet the other little girl. I wish I'd stayed to see that. It must
have been funny."

She irritated Everton by speaking exactly as if Monica were
a captive animal which had just been shown, for the first time
in its life, another of its own kind. The analogy thus conveyed to Everton was close enough to make him wince. He
felt something like a twinge of conscience, and it may have
been then that he asked himself for the first time if he were
being fair to Monica.

It had never once occurred to him to ask himself if she
were happy. The truth was that he understood children so
little as to suppose that physical cruelty was the one kind of
cruelty from which they were capable of suffering. Had he
ever before troubled to ask himself if Monica were happy, he
had probably given the question a curt dismissal with the
thought that she had no right to be otherwise. He had given
her a good home, even luxuries, together with every opportunity to develop her mind. For companions she had himself,
Miss Gribbin, and, to a limited extent, the servants. . . .

Ah, but that picture, conjured up by Miss Gribbin's words
with their accompaniment of unreasonable laughter! The

little creature meeting for the first time another little creature of its own kind and looking bewildered, knowing
neither what to do nor what to say. There was pathos in
that—uncomfortable pathos for Everton. Those imaginary
friends—did they really mean that Monica had needs of which
he knew nothing, of which he had never troubled to learn?

He was not an unkind man, and it hurt him to suspect that
he might have committed an unkindness. The modern children whose behavior and manners he disliked, were perhaps
only obeying some inexorable law of evolution. Suppose in
keeping Monica from their companionship he were actually
flying in the face of Nature? Suppose, after all, if Monica
were to be natural, she must go unhindered on the tide of her
generation?

He compromised with himself, pacing the little study. He
would watch Monica much more closely, question her when
he had the chance. Then, if he found she was not happy, and
really needed the companionship of other children, he would
see what could be done.

But when Monica returned home from the Vicarage it was
quite plain that she had not enjoyed herself. She was subdued, and said very little about her experience. Quite obviously the two little girls had not made very good friends.
Questioned, Monica confessed that she did not like Gladys—
much. She said this very thoughtfully with a little pause
before the adverb.

"Why don't you like her?" Everton demanded bluntly.

"I don't know. She's so funny. Not like other girls."

"And what do you know about other girls?" he demanded,
faintly amused.

"Well, she's not a bit like—"

Monica paused suddenly and lowered her gaze.

"Not like your 'friends,' you mean?" Everton asked.

She gave him a quick, penetrating little glance and then
lowered her gaze once more.

"No," she said, "not a bit."

She wouldn't be, of course. Everton teased the child with

no more questions for the time being, and let her go. She ran off at once to the great empty room, there to seek that uncanny companionship which had come to suffice her.

For the moment Everton was satisfied. Monica was perfectly happy as she was, and had no need of Gladys, or, probably any other child friends. His experiment with her was shaping successfully. She had invented her own young friends, and had gone off eagerly to play with the creations of her own fancy.

This seemed very well at first. Everton reflected that it was just what he would have wished, until he realized suddenly with a little shock of discomfort that it was not normal and it was not healthy.

V

Although Monica plainly had no great desire to see any more of Gladys Parslow, common civility made it necessary for the Vicar's little daughter to be asked to pay a return visit. Most likely Gladys Parslow was as unwilling to come as was Monica to entertain her. Stern discipline, however, presented her at the appointed time on an afternoon pre-arranged by correspondence, when Monica received her coldly and with dignity, tempered by a sort of grown-up graciousness.

Monica bore her guest away to the big empty room, and that was the last of Gladys Parslow seen by Everton or Miss Gribbin that afternoon. Monica appeared alone when the gong sounded for tea, and announced in a subdued tone that Gladys had already gone home.

"Did you quarrel with her?" Miss Gribbin asked quickly.

"No-o."

"Then why has she gone like this?"

"She was stupid," said Monica, simply. "That's all."

"Perhaps it was you who was stupid. Why did she go?"

"She got frightened."

"Frightened!"

"She didn't like my friends."

Miss Gribbon exchanged glances with Everton.

"She didn't like a silly little girl who talks to herself and imagines things. No wonder she was frightened."

"She didn't think they were real at first, and laughed at me," said Monica, sitting down.

"Naturally!"

"And then when she saw them—"

Miss Gribbin and Everton interrupted her simultaneously, repeating in unison and with well-matched astonishment, her two last words.

"And when she saw them," Monica continued, unperturbed, "she didn't like it. I think she was frightened. Anyhow, she said she wouldn't stay and went straight off home. I think she's a stupid girl. We all had a good laugh about her after she was gone."

She spoke in her ordinary matter-of-fact tones, and if she were secretly pleased at the state of perturbation into which her last words had obviously thrown Miss Gribbin, she gave no sign of it. Miss Gribbin immediately exhibited outward signs of anger.

"You are a very naughty child to tell such untruths. You know perfectly well that Gladys couldn't have *seen* your 'friends.' You have simply frightened her by pretending to talk to people who weren't there, and it will serve you right if she never comes to play with you again."

"She won't," said Monica. "And she *did* see them, Miss Gribbin."

"How do you know?" Everton asked.

"By her face. And she spoke to them too, when she ran to the door. They were very shy at first because Gladys was there. They wouldn't come for a long time, but I begged them, and at last they did."

Everton checked another outburst from Miss Gribbin with a look. He wanted to learn more, and to that end he applied some show of patience and gentleness.

"Where did they come from?" he asked. "From outside the door?"

"Oh, no. From where they always come."

"And where's that?"

"I don't know. They don't seem to know themselves. It's always from some direction where I'm not looking. Isn't it strange?"

"Very! And do they disappear in the same way?"

Monica frowned very seriously and thoughtfully.

"It's so quick you can't tell where they go. When you or Miss Gribbin come in—"

"They always fly on our approach, of course. But why?"

"Because they're dreadfully, dreadfully shy. But not so shy as they were. Perhaps soon they'll get used to you and not mind at all."

"That's a comforting thought!" said Everton with a dry laugh.

When Monica had taken her tea and departed, Everton turned to his secretary.

"You are wrong to blame the child. These creatures of her fancy are perfectly real to her. Her powers of suggestion have been strong enough to force them to some extent on me. The little Parslow girl, being younger and more receptive, actually *sees* them. It is a clear case of telepathy and auto-suggestion. I have never studied such matters, but I should say that these instances are of some scientific interest."

Miss Gribbin's lips tightened and he saw her shiver slightly.

"Mr. Parslow will be angry," was all she said.

"I really cannot help that. Perhaps it is all for the best. If Monica does not like his little daughter they had better not be brought together again."

For all that, Everton was a little embarrassed when on the following morning he met the Vicar out walking. If the Rev. Parslow knew that his little daughter had left the house so unceremoniously on the preceding day, he would either wish to make an apology, or perhaps require one, according to his view of the situation. Everton did not wish to deal in apologies one way or the other, he did not care to discuss the vagaries of children, and altogether he wanted to have as little to do with Mr. Parslow as was conveniently possible. He would have passed with a brief acknowledgment of the Vicar's existence, but, as he had feared, the Vicar stopped him.

"I had been meaning to come and see you," said the Rev. Parslow.

Everton halted and sighed inaudibly, thinking that perhaps this casual meeting out of doors might after all have saved him something.

"Yes?" he said.

"I will walk in your direction if I may." The Vicar eyed him anxiously. "There is something you must certainly be told. I don't know if you guess, or if you already know. If not, I don't know how you will take it. I really don't."

Everton looked puzzled. Whichever child the Vicar might blame for the hurried departure of Gladys, there seemed no cause for such a portentous face and manner.

"Really?" he asked. "Is it something serious?"

"I think so, Mr. Everton. You are aware, of course, that my little girl left your house yesterday afternoon with some lack of ceremony."

"Yes, Monica told us she had gone. If they could not agree it was surely the best thing she could have done, although it may sound inhospitable of me to say it. Excuse me, Mr. Parslow, but I hope you are not trying to embroil me in a quarrel between children?"

The Vicar stared in his turn.

"I am not," he said, "and I am unaware that there was any quarrel. I was going to ask you to forgive Gladys. There was some excuse for her lack of ceremony. She was badly frightened, poor child."

"Then it is my turn to express regret. I had Monica's version of what happened. Monica has been left a great deal to her own resources, and, having no playmates of her own age, she seems to have invented some."

"Ah!" said the Rev. Parslow, drawing a deep breath.

"Unfortunately," Everton continued, "Monica has an uncomfortable gift for impressing her fancies on other people. I have often thought I felt the presence of children about the house, and so, I am almost sure, has Miss Gribbin. I am afraid that when your little girl came to play with her yesterday afternoon, Monica scared her by introducing her invisible 'friends' and by talking to imaginary and therefore invisible little girls."

The Vicar laid a hand on Everton's arm.

"There is something more in it than that. Gladys is not an imaginative child; she is, indeed, a practical little person. I have never yet known her to tell me a lie. What would you say, Mr. Everton, if I were to tell you that Gladys positively asserts that she *saw* those other children?"

Something like a cold draught went through Everton. An ugly suspicion, vague and almost shapeless, began to move in dim recesses of his mind. He tried to shake himself free of it, to smile and to speak lightly.

"I shouldn't be in the least surprised. Nobody knows the limits of telepathy and auto-suggestion. If I can feel the presence of children whom Monica has created out of her own imagination, why shouldn't your daughter, who is probably more receptive and impressionable than I am, be able to see them?"

The Rev. Parslow shook his head.

"Do you really mean that?" he asked. "Doesn't it seem to you a little far-fetched?"

"Everything we don't understand must seem far-fetched. If one had dared to talk of wireless thirty years ago—"

"Mr. Everton, do you know that your house was once a girl's school?"

Once more Everton experienced that vague feeling of discomfiture.

"I didn't know," he said, still indifferently.

"My aunt, whom I never saw, was there. Indeed she died there. There were seven who died. Diphtheria broke out there many years ago. It ruined the school, which was shortly afterwards closed. Did you know that, Mr. Everton? My aunt's name was Mary Hewitt—"

"Good God!" Everton cried out sharply. "Good God!"

"Ah!" said Parslow. "Now do you begin to see?"

Everton, suddenly a little giddy, passed a hand across his forehead.

"That is—one of the names Monica told me," he faltered. "How could she know?"

"How indeed? Mary Hewitt's great friend was Elsie Power. They died within a few hours of each other."

"That name too . . . she told me . . . and there were seven. How could she have known? Even the people around here wouldn't have remembered names after all these years."

"Gladys knew them. But that was only partly why she was afraid. Yet I think she was more awed than afraid, because she knew instinctively that the children who came to play with little Monica, although they were not of this world, were good children, blessed children."

"What are you telling me?" Everton burst out.

"Don't be afraid, Mr. Everton. You are not afraid, are you? If those whom we call dead still remain close to us, what more natural than these children should come back to play with a lonely little girl who lacked human playmates? It may seem inconceivable, but how else explain it? How could little Monica have invented those two names? How could she have learned that seven little girls once died in your house? Only the very old people about here remember it, and even they could not tell you how many died or the name of any one of the little victims. Haven't you noticed a change in your ward since first she began to—imagine them, as you thought?"

Everton nodded heavily.

"Yes," he said, almost unwittingly, "she learned all sorts of tricks of speech, childish gestures she never had before, and games. . . . I couldn't understand. Mr. Parslow, what in God's name am I to do?"

The Rev. Parslow still kept a hand on Everton's arm.

"If I were you I should send her off to school. It may not be very good for her."

"Not good for her! But the children, you say—"

"Children? I might have said angels. *They* will never harm her. But Monica is developing a gift of seeing and conversing with—with beings that are invisible and inaudible to others.

It is not a gift to be encouraged. She may in time see and converse with others—wretched souls who are not God's children. She may lose the faculty if she mixes with others of her age. Out of her need, I am sure, these came to her."

"I must think," said Everton.

He walked on dazedly. In a moment or two the whole aspect of life had changed, had grown clearer, as if he had been blind from birth and was now given the first glimmerings of light. He looked forward no longer into the face of a blank and featureless wall, but through a curtain beyond which life manifested itself vaguely but at least perceptibly. His footfalls on the ground beat out the words: "There is no death. There is no death."

VI

That evening after dinner he sent for Monica and spoke to her in an unaccustomed way. He was strangely shy of her, and his hand, which he rested on one of her slim shoulders, lay there awkwardly.

"Do you know what I'm going to do with you, young woman?" he said. "I'm going to pack you off to school."

"O-oh!" she stared at him, half smiling. "Are you really?"

"Do you want to go?"

She considered the matter, frowning and staring at the tips of her fingers.

"I don't know. I don't want to leave *them.*"

"Who?" he asked.

"Oh, you know!" she said, and turned her head half shyly.

"What? Your—friends, Monica?"

"Yes."

"Wouldn't you like other playmates?"

"I don't know. I love *them,* you see. But they said—they said I ought to go to school if you ever sent me. They might be angry with me if I was to ask you to let me stay. They wanted me to play with other girls who aren't—what aren't like they are. Because, you know, they are *different* from children that everybody can see. And Mary told me not to—

not to encourage anybody else who was different, like them."

Everton drew a deep breath.

"We'll have a talk tomorrow about finding a school for you, Monica," he said. "Run off to bed, now. Good-night, my dear."

He hesitated, then touched her forehead with his lips. She ran from him, nearly as shy as Everton himself, tossing back her long hair, but from the door she gave him the strangest little brimming glance, and there was that in her eyes which he had never seen before.

Late that night Everton entered the great empty room which Monica had named the schoolroom. A flag of moonlight from the window lay across the floor, and it was empty to the gaze. But the deep shadows hid little shy presences of which some unnamed and undeveloped sense in the man was acutely aware.

"Children!" he whispered. "Children!"

He closed his eyes and stretched out his hands. Still they were shy and held aloof, but he fancied that they came a little nearer.

"Don't be afraid," he whispered. "I'm only a very lonely man. Be near me after Monica is gone."

He paused, waiting. Then as he turned away he was aware of little caressing hands upon his arm. He looked around at once, but the time had not yet come for him to see. He saw only the barred window, the shadows on either wall, and the flag of moonlight.

FAITHFUL JENNY DOVE

Eleanor Farjeon

Alack the day, alack the day
When my true love went away!
They killed my true love over sea,
And when they killed him they killed me.

I

When Robert Green, my true love, went to the wars, there was but one ghost in our village of Maltby. Now there are two.

Let me tell you. Jenny Dove is my name, and when I was sixteen years old they called me the prettiest girl in Maltby, though that is not for me to say. At all events, Robert Green, my true love, thought so; but then no doubt there was never a girl with a sweetheart who could not say the same; but then it was not only Robert Green; there were others; though for me there was only Robert. And when we had been plighted three short months, he went to the wars.

But I go a little too fast. I ought first to tell you of the Young Squire of Bride's Lane. We could not have told you in Maltby how far back his legend went; for all we knew, he had always been there. Many people had seen him, so they said, but none agreed about his manner of dress—one said he wore a coat of mail, one said he wore a ruff, another a frilled

179

shirt—so there was no judging when he had lived. But all
agreed that they had heard him weeping at break of day
beside the churchyard gate at the end of the lane by which all
the Ladies of Maltby arrive to be married; and as the sun
came up and touched him where he leaned against the gate,
he sank upon his knees beside it and melted away. For the
Young Squire was a morning ghost, and that's perhaps why
the details of him were hard to swear to—the black night
throws them up, but seen in daylight, a ghostly ruff or a shirt-
frill may be all one. I had never seen the Squire myself, never
in my life.

But the day my true love left me, I rose early and met him,
at his request, by the church porch, for he had a fancy to
stand at the altar with me and make a vow of constancy, as
binding on us both as marriage might be. We would have
liked very well to be married, but our mothers would not
hear of it, though I wanted but four years, and he but two, of
twenty. So he thought of this vow instead, and as I said: "If
love itself is not stronger than marriage, Robert, what use is
it at all?"

"Yes, Jenny," he said, "marriage lasts only as long as life,
but love lasts after death."

I thought this very true, as well as very poetical. Robert
was indeed a poet, and had written me some beautiful lines
for Saint Valentine, and also when my linnet died.

Well, as I say, we met in the early morning in the church
porch, before anybody was stirring, and as ill luck would
have it the church door was locked. This dashed us very
much, and we could not wake the verger, who was in charge
of the key, because he was my own uncle, and particularly
against Robert on account of his age, which indeed he could
not help, and time would remedy.

I could only just keep back my tears for disappointment,
and Robert looked serious, but was too manly to weep.

"What shall we do?" I asked, relying on his strength and
wisdom.

"We will pledge ourselves beside some other cross," he

answered thoughtfully, and glanced over the churchyard with its monuments.

But at this I shuddered. "Oh no!" not one of *those!*"

"Then come and stand with me by Eleanor's Cross," said he, and that pleased me better. Just outside the village was one of Queen Eleanor's Crosses where her coffin had rested, I forget how many hundred years ago. It was a husband's tribute to a faithful wife, and well suited to our purpose. The quickest way was by the Bride's Lane, and as we crossed the churchyard to leave by that wicket the sun was just rising. On reaching it we both looked up together and said in one breath, I, "Do not weep, Robert!" and he, "Jenny, you must not weep!" But neither of us was weeping in the least and the sun shone bright into the lane, where Robert and I looked too late to see anything. But we had both heard the weeping. I took it for an omen, if Robert did not, but I said nothing; and we walked down the Bride's Lane to the cross-roads where Eleanor's Cross stood on a grassy mound. There we took our oath, and what better words could we find than Robert's own:

"Marriage lasts only as long as life, but love lasts after death."

We each repeated these words, and then I added a promise of my own.

"Robert," I said, "until you return to me I will come every morning at daybreak to this Cross to watch for you; and here, where we now part, we will meet again."

"My faithful Jenny!" said he, and kissed me tenderly, and then I confess I melted into tears; but he said quickly, "Smile, Jenny, smile! You'll smile when we meet, let me leave you smiling."

So I managed to smile till he was out of sight. It was difficult, but it is wonderful what you can do.

The Wars lasted two whole years, and then the soldiers began to come back. During the first year I had had three letters from Robert, my true love, which were a great comfort to me. In the first one he said among other things, "How often I think of my faithful Jenny, smiling by Eleanor's Cross, as I last saw her. I have begun a ballad about you, or rather it is put into your mouth, as it were—the first bit goes:

> *Alack the day, alack the day*
> *When my true love went away!*
> *If he should die I will not wive*
> *With any other man alive.*
>
> *I stood there smiling in the light,*
> *The day my true love went to fight—*

but I cannot get any further with it. I would like to put in your white bonnet with the pink rose under the brim, and your pink frock with white frills, as I always see you. I think it will come out pretty if I can manage it."

In the second letter he said: "I cannot get on with the ballad, there is so much to do, but no doubt I will finish it one day."

In the third letter, which began: "My faithful smiling Jenny, do you still go every morning to the Cross?" he did not speak of the ballad.

Of course I told him I did so, rain or fine, wind, sleet, or snow, and all the village knew of it, and sometimes one or another who was out even came by to watch me, and the lads and girls teased me, though not unkindly, but my mother called me a silly. He did not answer this letter at all.

Then, as I say, there was peace, and the men began to come home, but not all of them, of course; and news took a long time coming, so there was much anxiety first, even when joy and not grief was to follow. But it is very strange how much hope there can be with anxiety, and every morning when I went to sit by the Cross, I was quite sure it was the day I would see Robert, my true love, come home from the Wars. And every day I came away, in spite of my heavy heart, I felt that there was always to-morrow to wait for.

And so another year went by.

Long before it was over they began to come and talk to me, sometimes kind and sometimes scolding. My mother said I was a fool to be wasting my chances, the girls told me to give it up, some of the boys came wooing on their own, and even my best friend, Mary Poole, talked gravely to me.

"Jenny," said she, "the War's been over for a year, and all the men that we know of are home again, and for a whole year before that even Robert's mother had no news of him. Jenny, you cannot go on waiting by the Cross all your life."

"Oh, Mary!" I said, "I promised I would."

"How long had you and Robert loved each other?" said she. "Scarcely three months—and how old are you now? Only nineteen. Why, you may live another sixty years!"

"That would be a long marriage," I said, "but not very long for love. Oh, Mary!" I said to her, "you do not know what true love is."

"I do, Jenny," said she.

"Who is it?" I asked.

But she was silent.

"And can you, then, Mary," I said, "bid me not to go to the Cross?"

She bent her head and went away without answering.

Then my mother went to his mother, and his mother came to me.

"Jenny," said she, "you're a good faithful girl, as so pretty a girl need seldom be. I'll own I mistrusted you when you were younger, for looks like yours might catch a lord. But I'll say now, if Robert came home I'd give him to you with my blessing. But he won't come home, Jenny; and I'll give you my blessing the day you go to church with another."

"I'll wait to go there with Robert," I said.

Then for a little they left me in peace.

Just a year after the ending of the Wars, I went to the Cross as usual. It was a lovely spring morning, and the larks were going up, and the grass round Eleanor's Cross was blue with speedwell, and it was easy to be full of hope; so when, as I sat there, a soldier came limping along the road, it did not surprise me in the least. I sprang up and looked towards him, smiling with all my heart. However, it was not Robert, my true love.

He was a much older man, about thirty years old, greatly hurt by the Wars, as well as lame. He came very slowly to the Cross and stood before me, looking me up and down. I waited for him to speak, but the words seemed hard to him.

"So you're here then, missy," he said at last.

"Yes," I said.

"Jenny Dove, are ye?"

I said "Yes," again.

"I've a message for ye," he said.

"Tell it to me," I said.

" 'Tis written," he said.

"Oh is it a letter?" I said.

"Nay," he said, " 'tis the end of a song."

Then he handed me an old bit of paper, very soiled, and on it was written these four lines:

> *Alack the day, alack the day*
> *When my true love went away,*
> *They killed my true love over sea,*
> *And when they killed him they killed me.*

The writing was very bad, but of course it was Robert's.

So I smiled at the lame soldier in the light.

On my stone in the churchyard they have cut the words:

JENNY DOVE
WHO DIED OF LOVE.

II

The morning after my burial, I rose early as usual. During my short illness I had been obliged to miss a few sunrises at Eleanor's Cross; it could not be helped. But after this I did not miss one; or yes, just one—and even then, in a way, I did not; but that will come later.

It was scarcely a week since I had met the lame soldier by the Cross, and if any morning could have been lovelier than that one, this was. I was in good time, so I took the long way over the Glebe Farm and through the village. The Glebe meadows were full of flowers. It is a beautiful thing to walk through flowers. No, I do not mean to walk among them, but to walk through them. They pass through your feet, and for a moment your feet and the flowers are one. Some of their sweetness is left in your feet from the daisies and primroses, and if your steps are happy, no doubt some of your joy remains with the flowers. In the copse I found a bed of violets, and lay on it so that I was filled from top to toe. I found it was so with all things. Trees and hedges and houses can all be a part of you; indeed, wherever you are, you become for that time the thing you pass through; nothing is lovelier than a bird flying through your heart.

It was the same with people. You could be closer to them than when you were alive. It was a pleasure to run among the school children as they came out of school. I walked with my friends when they did not know it, and every day I sat in the same chair with my mother. If a person is sad you can carry a shadow away from her heart as you pass through her, and if you are happy you can leave your own light there.

In buildings, too, and things that grow, you feel whatever life has left there. I always knew when joy or pain had filled the hands that laid the stones and raised the rafters, what the lives had been of those they sheltered afterwards; I always knew where men had quarrelled in the market, and where lovers had met in the woods. But now and then as I went about I lit upon something I could not understand—something sweeter than life, that had been left beneath a tree or in a flower. If it was a mood, it seemed finer than any mood shed from the bodies of things and creatures. Whenever I discovered it my spirit grew twice as happy as it had been, yet who or what had left it there I could not imagine.

I was glad to be a morning ghost, for it was only during my little vigil by the Cross that I could be seen, and then not by everybody; after that I was free for the day, and not visible at all, so that I could go where I pleased and startle no one. The night ghosts are less fortunate, for, as I once said, the dark shows them up so, and it is a sad thing to be feared. Besides, for some reason which I do not know, most of the night ghosts have sorrows. I had none. My only duty was to sit for half an hour in the morning by the Cross, smiling as the sun came up. This was all due to Robert, my true love. Thanks to him, I was a smiling ghost. None of us can escape a little duty, and mine could not have been lighter. Early as it was, a waggoner passed sometimes, and in the fine weather, if I looked down the west road, I would often see Mary Poole, crossing the pastures to turn out the cows. Many ghosts long for nothing but to be laid, but I did not wish to be; why should I? I had never while I lived had such delight in the world. I knew that had I died and Robert lived, I should have haunted the Cross only till he came home, and then I should have rested quiet in my grave. But now that could not happen, for Robert was dead, and I would always haunt the Cross. I took to saying the little verse the soldier gave me, every morning as the sun rose. I had little enough to do, and it seemed in keeping to repeat it:

> "Alack the day, alack the day
> When my true love went away!
> They killed my true love over sea,
> And when they killed him they killed me."

Besides, it was quite true. But I never stopped smiling as I said it. Many of the villagers said they had seen me, and one or two of them really had. And Mary Poole once heard me. I found her standing by the Cross one morning when I arrived. She was looking up the road and did not see me, so I sat down behind her, and when the sun came up I said my piece. She turned and looked at me, and grew pale, and said nothing. So I sat smiling at her till it was time to fade.

The only thing was that sometimes I felt lonely. You would think this was not possible, seeing that at any moment I could become a part of a beech tree, or a young lamb, or a crop of barley, or the busy road, or Gaffer Vine's warm chimney-corner. Still, it was so. I would have been glad of some one to talk to.

One morning in July I was a little late. I cannot think how

I came to oversleep myself, but when I stood beside my
headstone plaiting my hair, I saw by the sky that I would not
have time to go by the Glebe and the village, where I loved
to pass through the rooms of my sleeping friends. So I ran as
quick as I could to the little wicket that opened on the
Bride's Lane, a way I had not taken since I died. As I hurried
down the lane I saw the Young Squire hurrying up it. It is a
funny thing, but I had quite forgotten him till now.

They are all wrong about his dress. He wears a green
jerkin, and his face is most beautiful. He is twenty years
old.

When he saw me coming he waved his hand, and cried:
"Jenny Dove, who died for love?"

"Yes, Young Squire," I said, "but I am in such haste—
please do not keep me now."

"Ah, Jenny, thou'rt a young ghost yet!" said he. "How
could I keep thee? Pass, child, pass—but meet me at seven in
the Withybed."

So we ran straight through each other—but oh dear, the
confusion of it! I never felt anything like it. For when you
mingle with a solid body it is different; you seem to become a
part of that thing, rather than it becomes a part of you. But
when you mingle with a ghost like yourself there is no telling
which is which. For one instant I felt quite lost, I did not
know where or who I was, or if what I had been would ever
come out of that wilderness. And when I'd slipped through, I
was indeed not certain how much of me was left behind, and
how much of him I had carried away. I was only just in time
at the Cross that morning, and the half-hour went very slow.

When it was over, I went back to the churchyard to watch
the clock, and at last it wanted but fifteen minutes to seven.
So I thought I would go to the Withybed and finish waiting
there, and I did, and as I reached it saw the Young Squire
coming, too; we were both ahead of time.

We sat down together in the willow herb, and looked at
each other.

"Pretty Jenny," said he, "I have not seen thee these three
months, not once since they laid thee in thy green grave. But

I have heard of thee, and often found thy traces in the fields and the spinneys."

"Do *I* leave traces, Young Squire?" I asked.

"Wherever thou goest," he answered.

"And do you, too?"

"I too, wherever I go. Why, Jenny, what dost thou think? That bodies can leave their spiritual signs, and spirits cannot? Ah, Jenny, it's the spirit's spirit leaves the sign of angels on the earth—or of fallen angels."

I considered this for a while, and then a thought struck me. "Please move a little, Young Squire," I said.

He did so, and I instantly sat where he had sat. In the willow herb, whose rosy sprays had stood within his heart, I recognised the delicate trace which had so puzzled and enchanted me wherever I had found it.

"*You* do not leave the sign of fallen angels," I said, and held my hand out to him, smiling. He laid his own on it, and I could not tell which was which.

"Jenny," said he, "these three months I have found thy smiles left wherever the spring was sweetest, and I have tried to find thee all day long. For day ghosts are rare, and I have had some hundred lonely years. I knew it was thy task to smile at dawn by Eleanor's Cross; but unfortunately I must weep by the Bride's Wicket at precisely the same hour, and hasten to the Cross as I might at the end of my task, thou wert always gone. Let us not lose each other again, Jenny."

I told him we would not, and we agreed to meet in the Withybed each day at seven. It promised great happiness for both of us.

So ten years passed by, and we were as happy as we thought to be. For if one alone can take joy in the world's beauty, how much more can two together! And the joy was not of the living, who fears death to-morrow; the joy was endless, that fear was not for us.

Ghosts, I must tell you, seldom ask questions. What was, matters so little, what is, so much; only our small daily tasks bound us for a few minutes to the lives we had left, and when those were finished we had no cares for our own, or curosity for the other's past. Our working hours being the same, just what each did was never seen by the other, and, as I say, we were not curious to ask.

However, a few years after our first meeting it happened one Sunday that we went to church together, for it was the day I had died, and I wished to sit with my mother in her pew. And when the service was ended, and the church empty, we wandered through it looking at this and that, and by the old tomb where the Crusader and his Lady lay, the Young Squire halted, looking very kindly on the almost faceless figures. Suddenly he laughed.

"Jenny," he said, "lie there upon my Lady's effigy."

So I did as he asked, enveloping the stone form with my own, and felt strangely as he stood over me, looking down at me with the look I loved most.

"Yes," he said, "thou art fairer than she was."

"Oh, did you know her?" I asked.

"I died for love of her," he said. "I was Squire in her father's house, and we loved in secret, and my love was my passion, but hers was her pleasure. Then this knight came back from the East, and wooed her, and she was willing; and she summoned me to one last meeting, and as she lay in my arms told me with light words that this was the end. And I cried out that there might be an end to a woman's love, but there was none to her faithlessness, and left her. And the day she was to be married I sat and wept beside the wicket through which she must pass, and as the sun came up I swore to haunt that spot until one woman should prove faithful; and then I slew myself, where she and this knight found me later on. Cannot our pain make fools of us, Jenny? And so we die for love, which we should live for." He smiled at me, and we went out of the church together; and as we crossed the graveyard he stopped beside my grave, and read the stone.

"You also died for love," said the Young Squire. "To whom were *you* faithless, Jenny Dove?"

Oh, do you know how a shadow crosses a sunny field? Would you think such a shadow could fall on a smiling ghost, as I was? Yet it did. All of a sudden I feared to tell the Young

Squire my story; I feared to tell him I was faithful to Robert Green my true love, killed in the Wars. For then, you see—

I hung my head.

My Young Squire laughed at me, and said as he often did: "Oh, Jenny, thou'rt a young ghost yet! So young, thou canst still feel shame! and I'm so old that I can no longer feel bitterness. Smile, Jenny, smile!"

But if you will believe me, when he said this the tears ran down my face, and he looked at me in surprise, for he had never seen me weep before. Then suddenly he gaily laughed again, and ran in on me and stood over me, and surrounded me, so that once more I did not know myself from him, or my tears from his laughter, but in that wonderful confusion I heard his voice, merry, sweet, and teasing—

"Pretty Jenny! Smiling Jenny! Faithless Jenny!" he said, did my Young Squire.

When I heard him call me "faithless" I laughed too, and ran out of him, and he after me. It was a great game, the chase, the slipping through, the capture that could be no capture unless I wished—until such time as I did wish and stood quite still. We played that game often after this. And often he teased me for my story, and asked me what I did by Eleanor's Cross, and for what sin to love I was condemned to smile—he teased me for the pleasure of making me hang my head. But I did not weep again; why need I, seeing I had resolved never to tell him my story?

Then the tenth year passed by, and I went on a spring morning to Eleanor's Cross and sat and watched the road. And just before the sun came up, along the road, as it might have been ten years ago, came a limping soldier, of thirty years old. But this time it was Robert Green, my true love, home from the Wars.

III

As soon as he saw me he cried: "Jenny! Jenny! Faithful Jenny!" and came limping to the Cross. He held out his trembling hands that seemed afraid to touch me.

"Jenny, to find you here!" he said. "My Jenny, you have not changed a hair—but you're prettier, surely! And see, 'tis the pink gown and the white bonnet, as of old! and see, you're smiling still! To find you here where I left you, smiling still!" He buried his face in his hands. "Oh, say a word to me, my love," he sobbed.

But I could not speak.

He mastered himself and looked at me earnestly.

"Jenny, I've startled ye," he said. "Yes, thoughtless that I am. You believe me dead, because I was so long a-coming—and maybe you had my message that I wrote on the battle-field when I truly thought I was dying, and gave my wounded comrade to bring to you, if he should be luckier than me. Did you have it, Jenny?"

I nodded.

"My little love! it might have broken your heart."

"It did, Robert." They were my first words to him.

"Oh, cruel—but I'll mend it for ye, Jenny. But do not look at me so strange, see, it is myself in very faith, feel this hand, Jenny, indeed I am no ghost."

"But I am, Robert."

He looked at me as though he did not understand, then opened his arms and flung them about me, and then, poor man, he threw himself upon the ground by Eleanor's Cross with his face in the grass.

The sun came up just then, so I said my lines:

> "*Alack the day, alack the day*
> *When my true love went away!*
> *They killed my true love over sea,*
> *And when they killed him they killed me.*"

He lifted his face from the grass. "God help me!" said Robert Green, my true love.

"Robert," I said, "do not grieve so, there is less to grieve for than you might fancy."

"Yes, that's true," said he, "for do you remember our vow? 'Marriage lasts only as long as life, but love lasts after death.' I need not ask ye if ye remember it, my pretty love; have ye not kept faith after death itself? Ah, Jenny, if ever a woman was faithful, you are she!"

As he said these words the shadow fell upon me, the shadow I had felt five years ago. Suddenly it seemed to me that I could smile no more. And looking over Robert's head where he knelt in the grass at my feet, trying, poor soul, to kiss them, I saw the Young Squire standing with sorrow in his eyes.

"Alas!" I cried, "what has brought you here now, when you should be at your weeping?"

"Jenny," said the Young Squire, "when I came up the Bride's Lane this morning, I felt I had no cause to weep; I leaned on the wicket, and no tears came; I could not understand it; I ran to find thee—and how do I find thee! See, with thy true love at thy feet, praising thee as the only faithful woman among women! Ah, Jenny, how hast thou deceived me!—God help me, I fear I am laid!"

He turned and fled away, and oh, if a ghost's heart could have cracked, mine would have then.

But Robert, who had not heard him, but only my question—love giving him eyes and ears for me, which no others had; yet giving him none for other ghosts than me—Robert with worshipping eyes also answered me.

"What brings me here, but you?" he said. "And as for weeping, I'll be at that no more. See, Jenny, death need matter nothing to us; I'll keep troth with you by the Cross each morning till I die. Even if I may not touch you, I can see and speak with you, and that half-hour of love's sweet looks and words will carry me through each day. Smile, Jenny, smile, for love lasts after death!"

But I could not smile, for even for him I saw no happiness.

"Dear Robert," I said gently, "that's a vain dream. Have you forgotten to what I pledged myself when thirteen years ago we parted here? I vowed to watch each dawn beside the Cross till you returned again. Your death and my death could not break my vow—but see, my dear, you have returned, and I shall watch no more. God help me!" I sighed, "I fear—I fear I am laid."

"Jenny! you will not leave me—you will come again!"

"It will not be in my power, Robert," I said. "In a few minutes, this, my last vigil, will be ended, and I must go."

"Is there no hope?" cried Robert. "Of what use was it to come home to you, only to lose you? Oh, Jenny, is there no way?"

I thought and thought; and then, at the end of the west road, I saw Mary Poole passing to turn out the cows. Robert's back was towards her and she went without his seeing her. I thought suddenly there might be hope.

"Robert," I said, "were you true to me all these years?"

"As true as your own self," he said reproachfully. "How can you ask?'

"It might have changed things if you had not been," I said. "I am not certain—but, Robert, if you had been faithless, I might still have been allowed to lie unquiet in my grave; I might still have come each morning to the Cross, where we pledged our love; and for the sake of that broken pledge, I might have said at sunrise:

> 'Alack the day, alack the day
> When my true love went away!
> My love a faithless love was he,
> And when he broke his faith, broke me.'

They are not such pretty lines as yours, dear Robert, but they might have served—if you had been a little faithless."

"But I was not," said Robert obstinately.

"But you might be," I said quickly.

"Never!" he vowed.

"Robert, listen," I said. "I have only a moment now. Listen with all your heart. Life is life, and death is death. You will find that death can end no love that has ever been, and that love is one and also many, and none the less true for that. Well, this is for after death. But life must be lived, not wasted. While I am a memory you still have powers to be used till you become a memory, too. And there are those you might use them with, Robert, those that need them, as you will need—theirs. Indeed, there are many powers in life that cannot be used alone. And as we find beauty, as fair and sweet not only in one flower, so we may find love as true and pure not only in one woman. Dear Robert, my time's short—promise me one last thing."

"Anything, Jenny!"

"Do not show yourself in the village to-day—let no one know you're home until to-morrow. And come at day-break to the Cross again."

"Will you be here?" he asked.

"I'll try to be," I said; and then I faded.

I did not know how it would be at all—for me, for Robert, for Mary, or the Young Squire. But all that day I was so restless, it seemed to me I could not lie quiet in my grave that night, and if it was so with me, might it not be so with him? But I had no means of knowing, for I saw him nowhere.

Next morning, to my joy, I rose as usual. I knew I was being given one more chance. I dressed my hair my prettiest, and pulled out my frills, and tucked the rose under my bonnet-brim just where it showed its best. Then, full of hope, I sped, not to Eleanor's Cross, but to Mary Poole's bedroom.

She was still asleep. I saw how tired and sad she looked, and older than her thirty years. Oh dear, dear me! I sat down by her mirror, and pulled the little curls round my ears, and tied my sash again. Then I waked her. She did not know why she waked, or why she rose, and dressed herself, not in her old print, but her white lawn. She did not know why she stopped to gather six sweet violets and one dewy leaf from the bed by the path where they grew blue each spring. She did not know why, when she came to the end of the west road, instead of going straight across to the pastures she turned up it to Eleanor's Cross. But she knew—she knew who it was that waited there. She knew as well as I.

"Robert!" she cried, and went as white as a ghost.

He looked up quickly, but quicker still I had entered Mary Poole, who was my best friend, and stayed there, looking my prettiest and kindest at him.

"Mary!" he stammered—"I thought it would be Jenny."

Her eyes filled with tears, and she said, "Our Jenny died."

He came to her and took her hand. Oh, then I looked at Robert Green, my true love, with all my love, through Mary's tears. She never would have looked so, had she known it. Suddenly Robert took her in his arms and kissed her. How could he help it?

Then I slipped through her, through his arms, and him, so that neither saw me, and I looked at her and him; and she looked no more than one and twenty, and prettier than she had been at that age, and he looked not much older, and very tender. For, as I said, you leave what is in you with those you pass through.

I did not wait to see more—this was the one day I spoke of, when I neglected my task. I ran as fast as I could up the Bride's Lane, and there, oh joy! was my Young Squire, by the wicket, weeping his heart out.

He had just finished, as I came up.

"Jenny-all-smiles!" he cried, "why art thou smiling so? Tell me, why am I here and not resting in my grave? And why art not thou?"

"Oh Young Squire," I said, "how can I rest in my grave when Robert Green, my true love, is false to me? And how can you in yours, when I am false to him?"

I heard him say, "Pretty Jenny! Smiling Jenny! Faithless Jenny!" and then began the game of catch.

Mary and Robert have six blooming children and a little farm. It is a happy life. Sometimes they come of a morning to chat with me during my vigil, when I've nothing to do till the sun comes up, and I say my piece:

> *"Alack the day, alack the day*
> *When my true love went away!*
> *My love a faithless love was he,*
> *And when he broke his faith, broke me."*

As I said, we all have our duties, and none could be lighter than mine. Then I am free to go to the Withybed.

It is a happy life.